MISADVENTURES

WITH A

BOOK BOYFRIEND

BY
VICTORIA BLUE

MISADVENTURES

WITH A

BOOK BOYFRIEND

BY
VICTORIA BLUE

WATERHOUSE PRESS

For David —
the best boyfriend a girl could ever dream of having.

CHAPTER ONE

I was Oliver Connely, for Christ's sake! A household name—especially if the house had women living in it. For the past decade, my face had been plastered on billboards and buildings around the world and every magazine cover from *GQ* to *Esquire*. I'd walked for top designers in Milan, Paris, and New York. I was at the top of my modeling game.

But today?

Today I could barely pay my rent.

I'd heard of the proverbial "wall" from others in the industry but smugly laughed it off, never believing it would happen to me. After all, I was the most sought-after model of my generation. But my twenty-seventh birthday loomed like a dark cloud on the horizon, and the blustery wind that blew in before the storm took all the modeling jobs out to sea with it.

And now I was the guy scraping together change to pay his fucking cell phone bill.

Well, my agent, Harrison Firestein, might not be calling, but my favorite lounge chair at the pool in my condo complex certainly was. I'd been setting up shop there a few times a week to perfect my tan, relax, and forget about the stress in my life.

Since I actually *was* expecting a call from Harrison, I made sure my phone was charged and then grabbed my backpack and strolled across the complex to the pool.

I usually had most of the place to myself during the week. Everyone in Southern California was so health conscious and worried about wrinkles that sun worshiping had fallen prey to self-tanners and fake 'n bake salons. But I'd grown up in rural Iowa, where the summer was barely a quarter of the year and not a decent four-fifths. I hadn't yet given up appreciation for how the sun warmed my skin and gave me a sense of peace like nothing else in my regular routine.

I usually worked out five days a week, but I took an extra day off this week because—*honestly?*—I just wasn't that into it. It was so much easier for me to get motivated when I knew I had a shoot coming up or a show to walk. Since my phone had been unusually silent, I lacked the drive to hit the weights. Where were the job offers from Harrison?

The pool was particularly busy, and I questioned if I'd mistaken today for a weekday when it was actually a weekend.

No. Definitely not.

Skye Delaney, my best friend and amazing roommate, had been out the door at five thirty this morning like she was every workday without fail. Her punctuality used to annoy me, but I'd learned to admire her for her dedication to her career. I might not like the asshole she worked for, but she loved what she did and made a great wage doing it.

We'd been best friends since sophomore year at UCLA, and she'd been my rock when my family abandoned me for dropping out—and also through the crazy ride of my modeling career. It probably looked like we should've just hooked up and called it done. Been there. Tried that. We had less sexual chemistry than the leads in a bad rom-com. We could laugh about it now, but at the time, it was a disaster.

As I surveyed the crowd at the pool, a vacant lounge chair near the deep end called to me from across the deck. Three little shithead kids were screaming "Polo" in the shallow end while one of their pals turned in haphazard circles randomly shouting "Marco" to coax out their clap backs. Who was the sadistic bastard that came up with that game in the first place? I sent up a mental *thank you* to the ingenious creator of the AirPods in my backpack that were about to drown out the racket.

A cluster of empty chairs just a few feet from mine could pose a potential problem if those kids took a break and decided to camp out there, but a quick scan of the rest of the pool-goers yielded a view of their mothers across the deck. Two were absentmindedly watching the game in the water; the other two were huddled together, obviously talking about something they didn't want the others to hear.

I loved people watching. I'd done a good amount of traveling in the last few years, and often times I was alone. Making up people's backstories had become one of my favorite pastimes. I didn't even try to get it right. I just tried to make it interesting.

My own parents were two of the most boring adults I'd ever met. They met in high school and had been stuck with each other ever since. When I'd come along as an unwelcome party favor from their senior prom night, any hope of leaving that small town and making something of their lives went down the toilet with the first flush of morning sickness.

If the rest of middle-class America were in the same boat, I'd have begged that sucker to pull a Titanic. In the stories I created, people were happy, had adventures, and made the most out of every day.

A nasally voice broke through I Prevail's rendition of "Blank Space" being belted into my ear canal. "Anyone sitting here?" Judging by the "annoyed mom" look on the woman's face when I opened my eyes, she had already asked more than once. I pulled the little white pod from my ear and gave my practiced grin.

"Oh, excuse me. I didn't realize you had— Hey, what is that?" She pointed at my AirPod.

"They're the new AirPods. Perfect sound without the bothersome cord. They connect to your phone or any other device by Bluetooth."

"Well, I'll be... Janine, check this out!" She looked over her shoulder to her three approaching friends. Apparently, the leader of the posse was named Janine.

The bedazzled word *Diva* on her impossibly white ball cap threw tiny rainbows on her friend's face and chest as she spoke to her. "Honey, don't point at him like he's a piece of meat. I'm sure he has a name. And I saw him the minute we walked in. You'd have to be unconscious not to." Janine gave me a conspiratorial wink, like we were sharing a joke at her friend's expense. Except, when I thought about it further, it was really at mine.

She pushed her way past her friend and offered her hand. "Forgive my friend here. She doesn't get out much. We signed her out for a few hours before the nurses came by with her medication."

I took the offered hand and turned it over to place a light kiss on the slope of her inner wrist, but not before noticing the enormous pear-shaped diamond on her ring finger. And I'm talking enormous, as in "my husband works like a dog and we never have sex, but he buys me whatever I want" enormous. The way her mouth hung open after I grinned at her reinforced my assessment.

"Pleased to meet you, Janine. Oliver—"

"Connely. Shit! You're Oliver Connely!" She stammered and stared, and I had to admit, the effect never got old. For all the emotional scars they'd dealt me, I was eternally grateful to my parents for the physical attributes they'd bestowed upon me. Gene pool for the win.

"I am." I grinned again, motioning to the ladies to make themselves comfortable in the neighboring lounge chairs. It was becoming clear we were going to be spending the afternoon together.

"You live here? In this complex?" Janine commandeered the seat next to mine.

"I do. I'm sorry, but I think you ladies have me at a disadvantage. You already knew my name, and now you know where I live. How about some introductions?" My Midwestern upbringing always went over big with the females.

In turn, they each introduced themselves. They reminded me of the cast of *Friends*, fast-forwarded about ten years. Janine was the obvious leader of the pack, the Monica stand-in. The original friend I met—the woman fascinated by my AirPods—was Beth. She was a nutritionist and Sunday school teacher, and she reminded me of my mom. She was so much like Phoebe with her peace, love, and happiness vibe, I found myself visually searching around her lounge chair area for an acoustic guitar. Beth and my mom would be fast friends—exchanging recipes and wistful stories about wanting to be grandmothers. Something my younger brother, Shane, and his former high school sweetheart turned wife were working hard at making a reality.

Lisa was the Rachel stand-in. Stylish and sexy, albeit a little dingy. She spent the better part of the afternoon sitting by the side of the pool texting on her cell phone. The fourth woman was Dani. She was quiet and distracted, and when she excused herself to use the restroom, the other ladies quickly leaned in to explain she was having trouble in her marriage and was having a bad day. I nodded sagely, as if I had any experience to draw from, and sat back in my chair, put my pods back in, and closed my eyes—universal signals that I was checking out of the conversation.

Thankfully, it worked like a charm. When Dani came back from the bathroom, Lisa joined the ladies on the lounge chairs, and even though I had my AirPods in, I held off playing music so I could listen to what they were saying. There was a perverse part of me that was intrigued with the female psyche in general.

For example, when I was a boy, I would eavesdrop on my mom's sewing club when they met at our house. Inevitably they would gossip about their spouses, and sometimes the conversation would get pretty blue. I had my first sex-ed class while hiding behind the sofa listening to Mrs. Levinson talk about giving Mr. Levinson a "blowy" and fingering his asshole.

Listening to her insist to the other women that didn't mean he was homosexual was priceless, even at the tender age of ten.

"You okay, honey?" Janine asked Dani.

"Yeah. I'm fine. I really just wish he'd leave. I mean, I don't think I'm out of line in thinking if my husband is going to keep fucking his massage therapist, he should just move out of our house, am I? I can barely stand the sight of him at this point," Dani spoke to the group.

"I agree," Lisa said, shaking her head in disgust.

I pretended to shuffle songs so I was able to watch their interactions with inconspicuous glances.

"Instead of making you witness it all. It's just not right." Lisa now faced Dani squarely to convey her support.

"Well, that damn prenup says if I leave, I get nothing," Dani said to the group, starting strong but slumping back against her chair by the last part of the sentence.

"Yeah, well, isn't your sanity worth more than his estate?" Beth asked Dani, seeming innocent but somehow wiser than she let on.

I sneaked a quick peek from behind my sunglasses at the group's reaction when silence sliced through the air. They were all giving Beth the death stare.

"Well, I'm just saying..." She shrugged and then looked out across the pool.

"Let's talk about something else. What are you guys reading? Janine, you always have something good to tell us about." Dani decided the group needed a new topic rather than her dead-end marriage, and like a cardiac patient on the receiving end of a defibrillator, Janine jolted several inches off her chair.

"Oh. My. God." She even clutched her heart to further illustrate my simile. "You will not believe the book I just finished."

"Was it that biker one? With the guy?" Lisa waved her hand in the air, trying to jog her own memory. "With the brother? The twin?"

"No. I finished that like two weeks ago. God, girl, where have you been?" Janine scoffed, wholly disappointed with her friend's lack of upkeep with her latest literary prince.

"I can't keep up with you. How do you read so fast?" Lisa shook her head in amazement.

"I'm obsessed! Once I start, I can't stop until I finish, even if that means staying up way past my bedtime." There was a mixture of pride and resignation in the woman's voice. I couldn't pinpoint which was stronger.

"What's this one about?" Beth pulled the brim of her enormous sun hat down a bit lower and then adjusted the seat back of her chair for the seventh time.

"This guy is definitely my new book boyfriend." Janine's decree was met by her friends' orchestrated harrumphs, as if they practiced the ensemble regularly.

"They can't all be your boyfriends," several of them said in unison.

"Why not?" their fearless leader argued.

Beth was the first to cave. "Okay. They can. Fine. Go on." Something told me that's how the conversations always played out.

Dani asked, "Is he rich?"

"Duh. Who wants to fantasize about a man who's just

getting by?" Janine looked at her over the top of her oversized sunglasses and continued. "Or a fat guy? Or a guy with a small dick and a bald head? I can get *that* shit at home."

The whole gaggle burst out laughing, causing half the people at the pool to turn their heads to see what was so funny.

"Oh my God, Janine, keep your voice down." Beth tugged on the brim of her hat again. "There are children here."

"Oh please. Those aren't children. Those are Marissa's monster multiples. I live right next door to those little savages, don't forget. And I've had to hear Marissa and her husband making the next batch. Every night they go at it in their bedroom—which just happens to share a wall with my dining room. You want to lose your appetite? Listen to Harlem panting while she rides his wild wildebeest across the finish line if you know what I'm talking about. It sounds like an animal is either giving birth or dying a cruel and unusual death when that man has an orgasm. Or I don't know... Shit, maybe that's her."

The women were in stitches by the time she finished, and I wasn't doing much better. I'd given up pretending I wasn't listening a while back, and seriously? The lady could have her own comedy routine at the local open mike night.

"Please forgive her. She's not always this outspoken." Beth looked to me with tears running down her cheeks from laughing so hard.

The other ladies, again in what seemed like a well-rehearsed chorus, said, "Yes, she is!" Which, of course, made them all laugh even harder.

When the laughter settled down, Lisa reminded Janine they were still waiting to hear about her latest book boyfriend.

She spent the next twenty minutes going into great detail about the hero of the latest best seller.

The hero was some sort of "alpha male" billionaire, whatever the hell that meant. He told the leading lady what to do—and she liked it. Hell! She fell to her knees and gave him a blow job because of it. He was a dick to every other man in the story, and that really got her hot and bothered. For that behavior, she had anal sex with him!

"Oh my God! I would pay good money to have a date with a man like that. Wouldn't you?" Beth asked the group.

"Absolutely," they all agreed.

"Even an hour or two. Just to feel important to someone," Lisa added on.

"Exactly!" Dani said emphatically.

Apparently, the book was part of a series all the women were familiar with. The "hero" sounded like an arrogant asshole to me, but the ladies were swooning, and I mean *swooning*, over every example of assholeness their friend told about the guy. Did shit like this truly turn women on? I would definitely have to check in with Skye about this over dinner.

Crap. Dinner.

"Ladies, I need to go." I heaved myself off the lounge chair and gathered my things while I explained. "I completely forgot I have to cook dinner, and my roommate gets very, *very* testy if she doesn't eat the minute she walks in the door."

"Are you for real, Oliver Connely?"

"Excuse me? Ma'am?"

"Cut the crap. And if you ever call me ma'am again, I'll knee you in the balls. I'm not that much older than you. You little shit." Janine was a firecracker for sure.

When I raised my eyebrow, I instinctively lurched back at the hips, protecting my family jewels, and rightly so. She playfully hiked her knee up so fast, if I hadn't protected myself, I would've been singing along with Bruno Mars in his typical falsetto and not massacring the notes like I normally did.

"I think what our overcaffeinated friend was getting at is you may be too good to be true. So handsome, so charming, and you cook? How on earth are you single?" Lisa asked.

"He just said his roommate was a woman. That doesn't exactly sound single, now does it?" Dani was quick to point out.

"Oh, it's not like that," I corrected. "Skye and I are really just friends. Nothing more."

"Mmmm-hmmmm," they all answered in chorus.

"No, really. And honestly, I just haven't met the right woman yet. I'm always on the road with work, which really doesn't make for good boyfriend material." I shrugged. I also wasn't interested in settling down. Not in the very least. My parents' miserable faces flashed through my mind. Not to mention the damage they bestowed upon yours truly, not so subtly blaming me for snuffing out their hopes and dreams thanks to being the unwanted teenage pregnancy. Yeah... definitely not settling down anytime soon. The world didn't need another adult child with mommy/daddy issues.

"Thanks for the enlightening afternoon, ladies. Maybe I'll see you around."

They all said some version of goodbye, and I headed back to the condo. I noticed I had a voicemail from my agent,

Harrison, and was furious. How had I missed the call? I'd had my phone on the entire time. *Fuck!* The damn AirPods were in my ears the better part of the afternoon. My heart pounded in my chest while the message played on speaker as I looked through the freezer for something to make for dinner. I sent up a quick prayer that it would be one of the contracts we'd been waiting on.

"Hey, Oliver. It's Harrison. I just heard back from the people over at Lagerfeld. They loved your test shots, but it looks like they had their hearts set on a model with black hair. I told them you would totally dye it, but they weren't interested. Said it wouldn't be organic or some bullshit like that. Honestly, I think it was that suit you were wearing. I think we need to update your portfolio. I know this amazing photog in the art distri—"

I cut the message off and threw my phone across the condo, where it smacked into the wall and fell to the floor. It spun in circles until it slowed and eventually came to a complete stop.

How fucking symbolic.

That was the third job I'd lost in the past two weeks. My birthday was at the end of the month, and it felt like they would be playing a funeral processional instead of the usual "happy birthday to you" bullshit. My career was fading before my eyes, and the number of candles on the proverbial cake had as much to do with it as the gray hairs I secretly plucked from my sideburns in the privacy of my bathroom.

I was drying up.

I was a has-been.

I would be twenty-seven in two weeks, with no idea of

what to do next.

I was finished.

CHAPTER TWO

"Oll, this is amazing. I have no idea how you do this."

My roommate, Skye, sat back in her chair, eyes closed, and savored the bite of Chicken Marsala she'd just shoveled into her mouth. You wouldn't know by looking at her—she weighed *maybe* one hundred and twenty pounds soaking wet—but the girl could eat like an NFL linebacker. Where it went once it passed through her mouth was like a magic trick.

I cared about Skye more than I had ever cared about another human. She was more my family than the people I shared DNA with. I would go to the mat with anyone who hurt her, and I would do whatever it took to make sure she was happy in all things. She was a good woman, a good human being all around. And I'd been all around the world. Literally. I was well aware there were very few women like Skye left. She's a treasure, and she deserved to be treated like one.

"How I do what?" I smiled with satisfaction because I already knew what she was going to say. I just wanted to hear it again anyway.

"You know what." She followed her impatient answer with her typical eye roll. "Cook this way. You have a natural skill, Oliver. I can't boil water without hurting myself. This takes talent." She stabbed another piece of chicken with her fork, but my next comment stopped her short, just before she put the bite in her mouth to chew.

"I didn't get the Lagerfeld contract." I had no idea what made me blurt it out like that, but things were just like that with Skye. We didn't have to pretend to be things we weren't when we were with one another. Her gushing about my ability to cook made me feel like I had to counterbalance the positive with a negative. Like "don't be fooled, ladies and gentlemen; he's not really that amazing." I scrubbed my hand down my face.

Skye's chair scraped on the floor as she stood up. She was at my side, pulling my arms around her waist and climbing into my lap whether I wanted her to or not.

"Tell me what's going on." She pulled my face level with hers. "Tell me, Oliver Mason Connely, right this minute."

"I hate you," I mumbled.

"No, you hate Jägermeister." She grinned her smug little grin as she pressed her forehead to mine.

Another biological wonder about Skye Delaney? The girl can drink like an NFL linebacker too. I made the mistake of getting into some random shot-pounding contest with her early in our college days, and she weaseled every embarrassing personal detail out of me, one shot at a time. By the time the night was over, I was praying to the porcelain god, and she was jotting down notes in a journal she now called "How to Make Oliver Twist." She used them against me at inopportune times like this very one.

Did I mention she's witty too? And clever? Like a little fox, that one...

"There's nothing to tell. Hop up." I swatted the side of her ass, trying to make her get off my lap. "I need to clean the dishes before it all dries on."

"Stop." Her tone was serious. "The dishes can wait. I want you to talk to me. Did your parents call? This is the way you get when you've talked to them."

"No. I haven't heard from them in weeks. But it would be just my luck to get a call right about now. My dad seems to have some sixth sense about my misery."

"Honey, there will be other jobs. Lagerfeld is a creepy old dude anyway. What's with the sunglasses all the time? Am I right? Totally not your style to begin with. You should be walking for Calvin Klein—Donna Karan—someone that people can really identify with. Not a guy who looks like he may or may not be wheeled in from Madame Tussauds."

The laugh that escaped my throat was so unexpected, I nearly toppled Skye right off my lap. I wrapped my arms around her to save her from hitting the floor and buried my face in her hair.

"Why do you always smell so good?"

"Because you always sleep with fashion skeletons who stay thin with ciggies, Ollie. You need to find a nice girl. Spend some time being a boyfriend. Being somebody's person. You're so amazing, so special. You have so much to give... Why are you keeping it all to yourself?"

"Okay. Now I'm really getting up to do the dishes. You sound like my mom, and that is where I draw the line. Up you go, Miss Skye Blue."

I stood up, placing her on her bare feet as I did so.

"I'll help you," she said around a yawn so big I actually heard her jaw crack.

"You'll do no such thing. You worked all day and you're exhausted. And that big hairy ass crack will have you back in the office at dawn, no doubt. Go take a bath, or whatever it is you do in there, and get some beauty rest."

She picked up her pumps from where she let them flop off her feet when she came in the door and, with them dangling from her fingers, turned back to watch me clear the plates from the table.

"Can I help you, my lady?" I swirled the dishtowel before me in a gallant gesture.

"Don't worry about the rent this month, 'kay?" She wouldn't meet my eyes when she spoke, pretending to fuss with a thread on her skirt. She knew my pride was already fragile at the moment.

Stacking dishes in the center of the table, I said, "You don't have to do that."

"I want to. I know it's been a few in a row. I just don't want you to stress. I make more than enough to cover it, and I don't want to talk about it anymore." With that, she went into her room and closed the door.

I felt like the biggest loser on the planet. My twenty-seventh birthday was looming, and I was depending on my best friend to pay my rent. And the worst part about it? She was right. My checking account was under a thousand dollars. My savings account wasn't any better. I was in deep financial shit, and I needed to come up with a plan.

And these dishes weren't going to wash themselves. If

I didn't come up with something soon, I'd have to parlay my suds skills into a full-time gig.

Most of the night, instead of sleeping, I stared at the ceiling. I made a list of ideas when I finally gave in and admitted sleep wasn't going to be happening. When the sun came up, I got on the horn with Harrison and proposed a few of my ideas. He shot most of them down before I could even finish my sentence.

"Harrison. Harr— Jesus Christ, man. You're not even listening to me." Frustration ate away at my usual good nature.

"Actually, I am, Oliver. I'm listening to you sound so desperate you're making me want to lose my breakfast. And I paid good money for that ancient grains and kale smoothie, so I'd like it to stay right where it is, thank you very much. Not to mention this suit, aaaannnnd the upholstery in my car. God, can you imagine that smell in this heat? I heard it's supposed to be a real scorcher again today."

His prattling made me finally snap.

"Harrison! Shut the fuck up for a minute and listen. Man, what was in that smoothie? Crack? You are wired worse than normal. I need to work. Like right now. I need income, Harrison. I don't care what it is. I will fucking walk for JCPenney if I have to."

"Oliver. Connely. You take that back right now." The lethally calm tone of his voice made me take pause. "Don't you dare say reckless things like that unless you are looking to retire tomorrow," he said. "God, please tell me you are not in public right now. Are you?"

"Calm the fuck down. Of course I'm not. I needed to get

your attention. I knew that would work." Even if only half of it was true.

"That was not funny, Ol-i-ver."

Shit. I knew he was serious when he said my name like it was three separate words.

"I have to pull over. I think I'm having a stroke. Hold on. Actually, let me call you back. I need to check my blood sugar and realign my chakras. Wow, that was probably the cruelest thing a client has ever said to me. I'll call you back." With that, he disconnected our call.

I banged my head on the wall of my bedroom.

Twice.

Fucking Los Angeles—so many divas. I was going to be waiting tables by the end of the month, and my prima donna agent thought the worst possible thing that could happen would be modeling for a second-rate department store. At least I'd be getting a paycheck. At least I wouldn't be depending on Skye to pay my rent.

I decided to make another list. I needed to figure what marketable skills I actually had besides looking good. What other jobs was I qualified to do? This was the exact thing my parents warned me would happen when I decided to quit college. And, because I was foolish and thought I had plenty of time left to work, I hadn't been smart about saving money for this inevitable outcome. So here I was, no job, no skills, and no one to blame but myself. Homeless and sleeping my day away with the other bums on the lawn of city hall looked more appealing than calling my parents for a loan or, God forbid, moving back to their home.

It had been ages since I'd stared at a blank piece of notebook paper. Big surprise—still as daunting and intimidating as it had been in college. I wrote the number one and got to work.

1. Handsome.

Currently, that wasn't doing much for me, was it? Number two had to be better.

2. Good manners. Charming.

All true, but how did I parlay them into something marketable?

3. Good lover.

Then I snatched up the pen, crossed out good lover, and wrote GREAT lover. Now, I know every dude thinks he rocks his cock, but I know I can deliver. Even the cute little preschool teacher I met in line one morning at Starbucks finally agreed to play hooky from her job and show me what was under her prim little schoolteacher skirt in a hotel room a few blocks away from where her substitute had the class on a field trip. And, just for the record, I got straight A's on *that* report card.

But how do I put *that* on my resume? With a bit of aggression, I scratched a swift line from one side of the paper to the other, obliterating number three.

"Deep breaths, Connely. You got this." I closed my eyes, leaned back on two legs of my desk chair, and tried to calm down. It really couldn't be that hard to switch career paths at my age. I was barely out of school. People did it all the time. Even at twice my age. One more deep breath and I let the chair fall forward to all four legs.

I abandoned the numbering and just went with bullet points. I could go back through afterward and flesh out the ideas into complete sentences.

- *enjoy talking with people—if they're interesting*

- *amazing fashion sense from modeling*

- *impressive wardrobe—see above*

- *body in top condition from modeling for the past nine years*

- *no addictions*

- *single*

Looking back over the list, I had to chuckle. I sounded like one of the main characters in the romance novels the women were swooning over at the pool. Unfortunately, it seemed that was about all I was suited for.

And then it hit me.

Like really hit me.

The conversation the women were having at the pool yesterday. They each admitted they would love a man like the one they read about in their books. Their "book boyfriends," they called them.

That was my answer.

I could be that man. *Whoever* he was.

Be a woman's book boyfriend. Even if just for one night. Treat her the way she wanted to be treated. By the Cowboy. The Mob Boss. The Billionaire. The Alpha Male. The Motorcycle Club Prez. The Professor. You name it, I could be him. Shit, with all the personal ad options on the internet, I could be him by tonight.

I could work out a fee of some sort. I wouldn't have to sleep with the woman—or maybe I could? If that's what she really wanted. All of those details could be negotiated. Off the record, of course.

The idea took root, and I couldn't contain my excitement. I needed to move on it before I got cold feet. But I needed information about all these book characters, and I didn't have time to read that many books before setting my plan into place.

The woman at the pool... What was her name? The one who brought the subject up in the first place.

Janine.

I needed her. She already said she was obsessed—her words, not mine. I could enlist her help and let this thing gain wings. She was probably a pretty good representative of the demographic I'd be targeting. If I pitched the idea to her and she thought it was gold as much as I did, I'd place the ad.

No.

Maybe I needed to sleep on it at least one night. Those women were a little more voracious than I was used to dealing with. Maybe I needed to really consider what I was getting myself into.

One trip down memory lane to the look on Skye's face when she told me she would cover the rent because I was a loser and had no income, and I knew I didn't need any feedback from Janine or any of the other women from the pool. I never wanted to feel that small and demoralized again. And it wasn't anything Skye actually did. In fact, she handled the situation while sparing as much of my dignity as possible. That was all on me. I stripped my manhood all on my own by getting into this position in the first place.

Enough navel-gazing. Time to move forward and do something about the mess I'd created. I downloaded a nondisclosure agreement that I would have each client sign before meeting them in person. Once they saw who I was, I didn't want anyone getting any crazy ideas about blackmailing me for money—that I didn't have—or going to the press.

My personal ad was listed by noon on two websites with an untraceable email address as the only contact option provided.

Dating websites letting you down?

*Real guys not measuring up to the heroes
in your favorite romance novels?*

What if you could date one of the men from your fantasies instead?

A real-life book boyfriend?

*Maybe a Billionaire Business Tycoon? Or a Cowboy?
Motorcycle Club President? Fireman? Superhero?
Racecar Driver? Sports MVP?*

Maybe you have your own story you'd like to come to life...

Book Boyfriend Inc. can make your dreams reality.

Hourly, Daily, and Weekly rates available.

Contact us today: bookboyfriendinc@gmail.com

After I posted it, I knew for certain nobody would ever use it. I'd just wasted my morning. Which was a good thing, because...really? Book boyfriend?

And then my email notification dinged.

My stomached lurched. I wanted to look but was so afraid to read the message that I ran out the front door and beelined to the pool instead. When I got to the gate and realized I didn't have any of my normal things with me, including a bathing suit, I walked back to my condo, checking repeatedly if anyone saw what I had just done, convinced I must have looked like I was losing my mind. Luckily, I'd left in such a panic that I hadn't locked the door, because I didn't have a key to let myself back in. Much calmer, I sat down in front of my laptop, pulled up the email account, and read the message.

The client requested a date with a character named Jason Riley from a series called Riley House. She was looking for a single meeting with drinks, maybe dinner, and she checked the "open for possibilities" option on the questionnaire. She requested to meet Thursday night, which, after a quick check of my calendar, gave me roughly sixty hours to prepare.

Deep breath in, then out. See? I could handle this. Now, to figure out who this Jason Riley dude was. Maybe Skye had the book. I checked the bookshelf in the living room but came up empty. I pulled up Amazon.com and searched for Riley House. The entire page flooded with options. Ebooks, paperbacks, audiobooks... What the hell was all of this? Why did so many of them have the same title? Seriously. How could this be so confusing?

The panic inched up my throat again. Was I out of my league with this romance novel stuff? Maybe if I checked in with Janine I'd feel better. One major hurdle there—I had no idea which unit she lived in. I decided to take a little field trip to the leasing office, remembering the coy smile the sales agent always had for me when our paths crossed. Time to cash in on number two on my list. Maybe it was a marketable skill after all. Time to deploy a little Midwestern charm.

Perfect! She was behind the desk inside the cool, air-conditioned office. I closed the door quietly, and she looked up from her computer monitor.

"Hi." Her smile was even and blazingly white. Typical Los Angeles perfection.

"Hi. I'm Oliver." I offered my hand in introduction.

She shook it with an overly aggressive grasp, and I tried to disguise my wince behind an awkward smile.

"I'm Meechelle. Can I help you with something? You live in unit one eleven, right?"

"Uhh, yes, I do. Umm, I was hoping you could help me find my friend. Her name is Janine. I met her at the pool the other day. Real character." I thumbed my fist over my shoulder toward the pool area, as if she wasn't familiar with the lay of the property. Regardless, my phony discomfort was reeling her in like the catch of the day.

I leaned across her desk a bit to imply a bonding moment between us. She ate that shit up too. Sometimes women just made it too damn easy. "This woman was a bit older than you and me, but she was really lovely, and I told her I wanted her to meet my mom when she was out visiting. And that's just the thing. She's coming tomorrow. And I didn't get the unit she was in. Can you tell me that? Michelle, right?"

"Meechelle. And I'm not really supposed to give out information like that. I could lose my job. And I really need this job until I start getting some callbacks, you know?" She looked around the doorway into the adjacent office. I followed her glance, not realizing there was another space attached to the one we were standing in. The last thing I meant to do was get her in trouble.

"Hey, listen, don't worry about it. I don't want to put you in an uncomfortable situation." I started backing away toward the door, knowing there was no way she was ready to see me leave so soon.

"I have an idea, Oliver. Why don't you leave your information with me? Do you have a business card or something? That way, if I happen to see Mrs. Peterman today—like, when she stops by to pick up the package that was delivered for her"—she pointed with an exaggerated motion to the large box in the corner—"I can let her know you're looking for her."

Smart girl. I reached into my back pocket and came up empty. I had run out of the house so fast, I hadn't bothered to grab my wallet. "Damn it."

"Here you go." She was at the ready with a Post-it and a pen. I had to admire her quick thinking.

"I really can't thank you enough. I'll put my cell number on here and my unit number too. If you see Mrs. Peterman, can you tell her that she could stop by? I won't mind. She doesn't have to call first. I should be home all day."

"I'll let her know." She was smiling at me in a strange way, like she was hearing something I wasn't saying. "So, I have to work until the office closes today. Is that going to be a problem?" she asked.

"With what?" I was genuinely confused.

"Well, that's until eight." Her wide smile started to drop.

"I'm not following." Truly, I felt like I had missed a part of the conversation.

"I thought you were just saying you wanted me to... You know what? Never mind. I think we just got our signals crossed. I'll just make sure Mrs. Peterman gets your message." Her face was transitioning from a dusty pink to a deep crimson before my eyes.

"Okay. Thank you." It wasn't until I had walked halfway across the complex before I realized Meechelle thought I wanted *her* to come over tonight when she got off.

Shit. I wasn't half the player I thought I was. I better brush up my game if I had any hope of pulling off this book boyfriend bit.

CHAPTER THREE

Janine's and my mutual excitement for Book Boyfriend Inc. had grown into a frenzy over a venti latte at the corner Starbucks on Tuesday afternoon. Apparently, she had dropped by the rental office just after I'd been there talking to Meechelle and came directly to my place, balancing an enormous package on her hip when she arrived.

I'd offered to carry the parcel to her apartment and then told her the main gist of BBI while we walked, and it was enough to pique her interest. She'd suggested we discuss the details over a cup of joe. By the time we'd left the coffee shop, we were as amped on possibility as we were on caffeine.

Back at her place, she'd raided her library and emerged from her spare bedroom with a stack of books as tall as her sun-visor-topped head. She said it was my homework for the evening. I thought she was joking until I looked closer at the top book cover.

Holy hell. What have I gotten myself into? was all I could think. I wasn't a big fan of reading in the first place, and there were so many half-naked men on the covers and spines of the books, I was afraid of what I'd find within the pages.

And now, the following evening in my condo's foyer, it was time to review my studies.

"Do you remember what I told you?" Janine's respect for personal space had gone out the window as she straightened the lapel of my suit for the third time.

"Yes. But stop asking me questions." I batted gently at her hands. "You're making me nervous."

"Oliver. Trust me." She dropped her hands but not her drill sergeant tone. "Women love these characters. They read the same book four and five times. Sometimes more. They know every detail about these guys. They know them better than they know their own husbands."

"Does any of that seem weird to you?" I couldn't help but laugh. But the deadly serious look on Janine's face quickly told me it was not a joking matter.

"Okay, so the client listed the character Jason Riley specifically," she said in a tone that was all business.

"You're familiar with this book, I assume?" I asked.

"Isn't everyone?" The word *idiot* was implied by her expression. "He is the alpha billionaire of *all* alpha billionaires. He's probably the one who started the craze in the genre, honestly."

"So what do I have to do? Tell me the main points of this guy. I'm the Skywalker to your Obi-Wan. No, better yet...your Yoda."

"You didn't read the books, did you? What was the first thing I said when you came to me with this crazy-ass idea?"

"I hope you can speed read," we recited in unison.

My neighbor just shook her head in disappointment. Her face morphed into my father's before my eyes. "You should've read the books, honey. He has so many one-liners, it's not really something I can just tell you about. Can you postpone the date?"

"I doubt that would be getting off on the right foot with the client. And I did read the book. The first chapter. Well, some of it. Okay...I skimmed a lot. Tried to stick to the dialogue mostly. Get the feel of the guy, you know? But Janine, let's be real here. There are like twelve books in that tower you sent me home with." Pacing seemed the only way to handle the nerves creeping up the back of my neck.

"*Oh!*" Janine's outburst made me jump mid-pace, and I bumped into the edge of the odd-shaped table in our entryway.

"It's perfect, actually. I can't believe I forgot this! Jason Riley always cancels appointments with his leading ladies. It makes them crazy. He's a workaholic. So, when the woman finally gets a few minutes alone with him, she feels like she's the queen of his world. And he usually makes every second count, if you hear what I'm saying." She waggled her eyebrows in case I didn't pick up the meaning from the words alone.

"Oh, I'm hearing you. So, it would actually fit the character to cancel?" I stopped pacing long enough to let the idea take root.

"Yes! But he's such a dick, he always has his assistant call. So, I'll pretend to be his assistant, Mary Jane. Do you have the client's number? Oh, this is going to be perfect!" She clapped her hands in front of her, her enthusiasm contagious. I found myself relaxing as if this was all part of the plan the entire time.

"You got so lucky she picked this book. I'm telling you, Oliver, you better read up on him tonight. You've got some big pants to fill."

"Isn't the saying 'big shoes to fill'?" I gave her a confused look while she dialed my first client's phone number.

"Not with this guy." She laughed.

I just shook my head, trying not to egg her on by laughing too.

Janine was a pro. I listened to her call my first date...and cancel it. I had a brief moment of panic—what if the woman got pissed and didn't reschedule?—but Janine handled that part too. By the time she disconnected the call, she'd scheduled another date for the following night. Same time, same place, and this time I knew I'd be better prepared.

My slightly crazy neighbor was right. I'd totally escaped disaster by the skin of my teeth. I would spend the rest of the night reading the story about Jason Riley, and in the next twenty-four hours, I'd become him.

"What's the name of the book this guy is in again?" I scrolled through my phone and pulled up a book retail site to purchase the material I'd be studying. If I had it on my phone, it would also be on my tablet, and then I could take it with me if I got a call from my agent. I could also highlight important facts, which I couldn't do in the books Janine had lent me.

"Oh, honey." Janine's pitying tone dragged my attention from the screen of my phone to her commiserative stare.

"What is that 'oh honey' crap? My mom does that when she's about to tell me something really shitty."

"It's not *a* book. It's *six* books." She reached out to rub my arm in consolation, but I yanked back out of her reach.

"*What?*" The word leaped from my mouth as if it had free will.

"Six. A series. *House of Riley* is a series of six books that takes place over a period of eight years. I *think*. Shoot, I don't remember exactly, but really, it doesn't matter. It's about Jason Riley's journey as a man, as he discovers what is truly important in life." The woman recited the book facts as if she were doing a commercial for the publisher.

Panic swelled up in my throat, squeezing my breath out in pants. "Janine!"—*gasp for air*—"I can't read six books in twenty-four hours."—*sucking in oxygen*—"I was already thinking one was pushing my abilities."

"Hey, sweetie, calm down. Here, sit down for a minute." She eased me to the floor, right in the middle of the entryway of the condo. "You look a bit pale, honey. Why don't you loosen your tie, take the jacket off? Here, let me hang it up for you."

I just did what she said. It was easier to listen and obey than to argue, as my brain faded back and forth from hazy to clear, oxygen not flowing easily due to the shallow pants I substituted for breathing.

"Oliver? Oliver! Breathe normally, hon, or you're going to pass out." Janine tossed my suit coat to the side and dropped down to her hands and knees in front of me, putting her face level with mine. "Honey, listen to me. Deep breath. Come on, breathe with me. In..." She took a dramatic breath in so I would follow her example.

In the middle of the impromptu Lamaze class, Skye came through the front door, right on schedule after a hard day at work. Originally, I had hoped to be long gone when she got home. Instead, an older-than-what I-usually-went-for woman was all but straddling my lap, right in the middle of our foyer.

My tie hung loosely from my neck, and my suit coat was thrown haphazardly on the floor behind us. And instead of explaining what was going on? We both froze with guilty expressions on our faces.

"Oh! Hi. Sorry. Sorry to barge in here." Skye began to apologize but changed tactics when she got a good look at my face. "Oliver? Oliver! Hey, are you okay?" Skye joined Janine on the floor in a flash. "What's going on? You don't look so good."

"I'm fine. I just... It was just..." At a loss for what to tell her, I just fell back on the floor and threw my arm over my eyes. I could hear the rustle of bodies shifting as both women stood up.

"What's going on, Oliver? Spit it out." Skye had the world's most accurate bullshit meter, and this was definitely not the way I wanted to explain my new income-producing strategy to her.

"Janine, you should go." I mumbled the words from behind my arm that was still slung across my face like a four-year-old who was about to get scolded.

"Are you sure you're going to be okay?" Janine was halfway out the door before she made one last welfare check.

I rolled up to a sitting position so she would feel better about my condition and move along. "Yeah, I'm okay. Thank you. For everything. I'll talk to you tomorrow, okay?" When she still lingered in the doorway, looking like she might start talking about the whole Book Boyfriend thing, I stood up and all but shoved her the rest of the way out the door. "Please. Just go. Seriously, I'm fine now," I pleaded with her through my stare, and finally she caught on.

"Okay. You have my number, though, if you need anything."

"I do. I appreciate it. And I appreciate your discretion with this whole situation, Janine. Like we talked about." A little reminder seemed in order.

I straightened my slacks and picked my jacket up when I came back inside while Skye closed the door behind me.

Thoughts swirled around my mind. I could have said I wasn't feeling well and gone to my room. Skye might've just left me alone and not asked any more questions. But that would have only gotten me through tonight. Eventually I would have to tell her what I was up to.

I considered lying to her, telling her I'd landed a new contract with a signing bonus. It wasn't very common these days, but some of the old-school agencies still did it. But Skye would definitely know if I had been shopping agents, and while I complained a lot about Harrison, I couldn't ask for a better representative in this ridiculous industry.

I needed to rip the Band-Aid off and just tell her my plans. Maybe she would be supportive. Maybe she would congratulate me for coming up with an innovative idea and help me think of some great marketing strategies.

Maybe Michael Jackson and Prince would pop out of my bedroom closet and break out in a rousing duet of "Man in the Mirror" and I would be inspired to find a cure for the world's food shortage.

"I'm just going to call it a day. I'm not feeling so great, and I'd hate for you to catch whatever I'm coming down with." I shielded my face from Skye with a big flourish. If there was one thing my best friend dreaded, it was catching something from other people—to the point of carrying hand sanitizer in every purse, briefcase, and desk drawer. She'd wear a surgical mask everywhere if people wouldn't stare at her—because she's afraid of that too.

"Oh no. Is that what was going on when I walked in?" She started backing away from me infinitesimally. She was trying to be sly about it, but I knew what she was up to. "Why were you on the floor?"

"Yeah, I guess. Just a dizzy spell." Shrugging, I tried to seem nonchalant about the conversation. "I've been off my game all day. Best if I just go sleep it off, I think." I felt my forehead with the back of my hand for affect. "Do I feel warm to you?" A few steps in her direction had her raising her hands in front of her in a full-stop motion.

"I'd really rather not touch you, Ollie. No offense, but I just can't afford to miss work right now. You understand, don't you? The election is right around the corner."

"Yeah, yeah, of course. I have a thermometer in my medicine cabinet." I rubbed the back of my neck and turned toward my own room. "I'll see you in the morning, hon."

"Wait. Who was that woman?" she asked curiously.

"Just one of the neighbors. Her name is Janine. Real nice lady. She and her husband live in the next building over."

"You're hanging out with the neighbors now? Christ, Oliver, next you're going to be in the Red Hat Society. Or scrapbooking." She laughed at her jab but still gave me a sympathetic look. Skye had a big heart under her ice-queen veneer.

"You know, if I didn't feel so shitty, I'd take you over my knee." I made the threat sound extra weak in my exaggerated sick voice.

"Mmmm-hmmm. I wouldn't make that threat too lightly around your new friend if I were you. She was looking at you like you were starring in her dreams last night."

"Sounds like *someone* might be jealous."

"You wish, Oliver! However, a decent spanking sounds pretty tempting right now."

My brows shot up into my hairline. "I'm not touching that with a ten-foot pole, young lady. Even if I weren't sick, I'd walk right on by." I knew my bestie was kinky, but there were things a guy just didn't want to think about.

"Yeah, better that way." The wistful look on her face lingered as I trudged toward my room.

"Exactly! Night, Skye Blue. Sorry I didn't make you dinner tonight. You and Sunny the Cocoa Puff mascot are on your own tonight."

"That's cool. You know I'm cuckoo for Cocoa Puffs." Her lack of enthusiasm was comically opposed to the slogan's normal delivery.

"Yeah, you are."

"Night, Oll. Feel better."

I closed my bedroom door and leaned up against it. I hated lying to her. There was no way she was going to be cool with me renting myself out to women.

But I couldn't dwell on that. I had a book to read. Make that *six* books to read. And one really important character to study. If this Riley guy was as popular as Janine claimed, I'd probably have other women requesting dates with him.

Getting comfortable with a stack of pillows against my headboard, I opened my tablet and dived into the *House of Riley*. The first book in the series turned out to be pretty decent. I could respect Jason Riley on a dude level. He was a guy I could see myself being friends with. He was a bit of an ass with the ladies, but for some reason, they ate it up. And every guy had seen it happen in real life too. Ladies love the guy who treats them just a little wrong. He gives them the "good" so damn good that they overlook the bad. The guy had all the moves in the bedroom, and because the book was written by a woman, it was all but a roadmap of how to please the fairer sex.

Come to think of it, if guys were smart—which, let's face it, we aren't—when we were about eighteen, we'd pick up one of these books and study it like it was one of our core subjects in school. We'd have the girls eating out of the palm of our hands in no time. This kind of book was all but giving a guy the code to the safe that was otherwise impenetrable. The female orgasm. Men work for years, sometimes a lifetime, figuring out what makes a woman get off, when all along, here it was, written, step by step.

And it wasn't just sex. The courting, the love language, the dirty talk, the navigating the family maze—all of it. I ended up reading until two in the morning, finally falling asleep after promising myself *just one more chapter*. I had a strange desire to talk to someone about the book I was reading, but waking up Skye seemed out of the question. It would have to wait until daylight so I could wait for Janine and the rest of the *Friends* gang at the pool.

I never heard Skye leave for work in the morning, which was highly unusual. She wasn't particularly considerate as she slammed around the condo getting ready in the morning, and I had always been a light sleeper, so the combo usually meant when she was up, I was up. But staying up late reading ensured I slept through her cacophony, and I didn't wake up until my cell phone finally rang at nine fifteen a.m., stirring me from a bizarre mix that was part sex dream part nightmare.

"—lo? Hello?" I mumbled into the phone, hoping whoever it was had something important to say.

"Are you really still sleeping?" Harrison's voice chastised me from the other end.

"I've been under the weather." Hell, the excuse had worked on Skye. Why not go for broke?

"Oliver." His dramatic sigh had me clenching my fists. "This can't still be about Lagerfeld." Why did he sound so put out when it was my career that was drying up?

"I just said I'm sick. There's something going around." A fake cough was added for bonus points.

"You should go get a colonic. It would do you wonders. I have a great therapist—"

"Please do not say another word about your colon, Harrison. Or having things pumped into you from down below. It's way too early in the morning. Is there a reason you're calling me?" If I didn't interrupt him, the granola medical advice would go on for the better part of his commute.

"Of course." This time the pause, just as dramatic, was way more self-congratulatory. "I have a job for you to go to today. Clean yourself up and be ready by ten. They're sending a car.

I emailed you the info, but when you didn't respond, I figured I'd better call and make sure you're *still* checking your email."

"Shit," I mumbled into the phone and instantly prayed Harrison hadn't heard me. God, could this be a sign? Maybe the dry spell was just temporary and I had misread the signs in my usual paranoid panic. Maybe this would be the start of the feast and the end to the famine. Maybe I could say goodbye to the likes of Jason Riley before I got too comfortable even considering wearing his shoes.

"My head is throbbing. I just didn't sleep well." Who would believe I'd stayed up too late reading?

"Too bad, Oliver. Fake it if you have to. This is LA, baby. And Oliver? You're welcome. I really had to pull strings for this one. Wear your navy Armani. It's my favorite on you." And he was gone.

I flopped my head back into my pillows and opened my email. The job was an easy one, at least. A few hours on location with a photographer I'd worked with before. The campaign was for a top-shelf vodka and was being shot at some trendy hipster place in the Financial District. I took a quick shower, skipped the shave per the client's request, and threw on some track pants. I'd have my hair and makeup done on-set and get into my suit at the last minute. I wondered why Harrison had to pull strings to land this gig. I'd done a hundred shoots just like it in my career. Grabbing my e-reader off my bed, I headed out the door. According to the call sheet, I should expect to be back home with plenty of time to get ready for the BBI date tonight, as long as the traffic gods cooperated during the afternoon rush hour.

CHAPTER FOUR

For the first time in my entire modeling career, a shoot had dragged on. Even though I had worked with the photographer before, every single nuance about his style grated on my nerves. The shots seemed to take an eternity to set up, only to snap a handful of frames and move on. My posing had been spot-on; some things truly were like riding a bike. The dailies I saw looked fantastic, and I was confident the client would have what they were looking for. Still, I couldn't have left the set fast enough. Where I used to feel accomplished and satisfied when a job wrapped, I'd felt uninspired and restless.

Over the lunch break, I'd found a quiet corner and read a few more chapters of the *Riley House* book I was so engrossed in. One of the lighting interns caught a glimpse over my shoulder of what I was reading, and we'd talked for a few minutes about the characters. Oddly, I had more interest in that conversation than in any other part of the day. We'd exchanged socials and agreed to keep in touch on something called Goodreads. Apparently, there was an entire platform and community dedicated to the love of reading. Who knew?

The photographer had gone way over time, and I'd ended up going straight to my date from the shoot. It all worked out since I had my best suit on and my hair was styled to perfection.

I met Melanie, as she'd listed her name, in the lobby bar of the Standard, one of Los Angeles's trendiest hotels. Also, as luck would have it, the hotel was in the same neighborhood as the photo shoot, so I didn't have to travel far and actually was early for the date. I had the pleasure of watching her arrive and fidget, while she wasn't aware I observed her from across the bar.

She was stunning. Nothing like I had worked myself into expecting over the past twenty-four hours leading up to this moment. And the fact that I had done that seemed so unfair now. Just because a woman chose a dating service instead of finding a date some other way shouldn't automatically check off boxes like spinster, cat lady, and dowdy. This woman was anything but those descriptors. Quite the opposite, actually. She was stylishly dressed and had an air of sophistication a woman couldn't be taught. No, a woman was born with this type of poise and grace. My body reacted to her in ways I hadn't felt in quite some time. I shifted on my perch of a barstool and chuckled to myself, surprised by the effect she already had on me before we'd even met.

We had drinks and great conversation, getting to know one another casually, all while I played the character to a T. She ate the shit up quicker than I could dish it out.

"I can't believe I'm doing this." She smiled shyly into my shoulder as I backed her farther into the dark corner of the hotel lobby's bar.

I leaned close to her ear, breathing heavy on her bare neck before whispering, "Why? Not one for adventure?"

"Not normally, no." Her voice was thickening with arousal,

much like my dick. The drinks and spirited atmosphere of the bar played right into the vibe of the scene.

"Maybe we should change that." Delivered with the trademark smoldering stare of her book boyfriend, Jason Riley. She melted within seconds and looked down.

"Don't do that, Melanie."

"Do what?" Her question was asked with a batting of her black lashes.

"Avert your eyes when I'm looking at you." I kept my voice commanding without being mean. Right on the edge of "Dickville."

"It's too much." She waved her hand. "Too hard to—"

"To what?" I volleyed back quickly like my character was known to do.

"I don't know. Never mind." She was blushing. I had her just where I wanted her.

"You're going to have to say what you mean. Say what you want—if I'm going to give you what you need, Melanie." I brushed a lock of silky hair behind her ear, letting my fingers linger on the shell.

I waited for her to look up again. Finally, when she did, I hooked my forefinger under her chin and bent closer to kiss her. Moving slowly, both to draw out the moment and to give her plenty of time to say no. Even though we were knee-deep in this role-playing, she had every right to tell me no.

When the kiss was finished, I pulled back. "That wasn't so bad, was it?"

Her lips trembled as she raised her hand to touch where mine had just been. Finally she spoke. "No, no, it wasn't bad at all. It's been so long since someone kissed me like that. Actually, I don't think I've ever been kissed like that."

"You deserve to be treasured, Melanie." I looked out across the bar dramatically like the actors did in the soap operas my mom used to watch. "But I'm not the right man for you."

"No!" she answered too quickly. "Why are you saying that?" She tugged on my lapel to get me to look back at her—as though she had watched the same cheesy soap opera scene too.

"I'm not a nice guy. I work too much." I was pouring it on now. She was putty in my hands.

"No, I want you. I want you just the way you are." Her voice broke a little on the last word.

"You don't know what you're saying." This couldn't have gone better if we'd rehearsed it.

"I'm a grown woman. I know what I want." She stood taller, resolve straightening her spine, as if a decision had been made deep inside.

"And what is that?" I looked her directly in the eye. "Tell me what you want, Melanie."

I felt something touch my hand and looked down. A plastic hotel room key card.

"I want to spend the night with you."

"Make sure you understand what that means. We can't go back in time once we cross the line." Subtle warning edged my tone.

"I want to be with you. Feel you." Her hands were roaming over my chest, inside my suit jacket, nails scraping my skin through the thin cotton of my dress shirt.

"Melanie," I rasped in her ear just before I sank my teeth into the lobe. Her moan was like fingers wrapping around my cock, a firm grasp as I kissed down her neck, and she let out a rush of warm air.

"Please, please. Take me to your bed, Melanie. I need to feel you."

She turned on her spiky stilettos and strode out of the bar and across the lobby toward the bank of elevators. I went closely behind, although keeping a respectable distance once inside the guest-filled car. On the eleventh floor, we both exited, and I watched her strut down the corridor of the hotel toward the room she must have reserved earlier. I waited a few moments before following in her wake. She opened the door but didn't turn to see if I had followed before going inside. I caught the door just before it closed and pushed it with a force that startled her. She watched with big green eyes as I prowled toward her, minimizing the space between us in two long steps.

"I-I don't know what to call you," she breathed as I kissed her neck.

"Do what feels right. You're in control of everything that happens here. If you want this to be strictly a fantasy, then so it shall be. You know my real name. We talked about that over dinner. I won't mind if you say that when I'm deep inside you either." I kissed down her neck again, trading stinging bites for soothing licks, holding her in place by her lithe waist. "Melanie." I held her still and waited for her to look at me. "Melanie, look at me."

"What? What's wrong? God, please don't say you've changed your mind." Panic filled her voice and stare.

"No. It would take every ounce of my will to walk out of this room right now. But I want to make sure you've had every opportunity to say no. If this is not what you want to be doing, say the word, and I will be a gentleman and walk out that door."

"No. God, no, Oliver, please. Make love to me. Fuck me. However you want to word it. I need to feel alive. I need to know I'm desirable. That a man could actually be attracted to me. Please, if only for one night. Make me feel special. Make me feel like I'm beautiful, that I'm needed. Wanted."

Her eyes were welling with tears, and her swollen lips trembled. She looked so vulnerable and lonely, I wanted to wrap her in my arms and hold her until the sun came up. But I knew she needed more than that. I kissed her again, letting my desire swirl through her system, replacing the doubt and fear that had crept in over the past few minutes. I pressed my erection into her soft flesh, making it abundantly clear how desirable she was.

"Feel what you do to me? You have the power to bring a man to his knees." I took her hand and wrapped it around my cock through my slacks. "You have the power to destroy me. Say you'll have me. Say you'll have me between these milky thighs." I slid my hand up under the fabric of her dress, pressing in at the junction of her pussy. "Say this is mine, Melanie."

Her green eyes glowed in the dimly lit room.

"Say it."

Her stare could've lit the way for a battalion of soldiers on a midnight raid.

"Don't make me ask again." This time my command was issued against her lips as I grabbed her pussy firmly in my palm, making her suck in air from my mouth.

"I can feel the heat from your cunt. You like when I tell you what to do. Don't you?"

She nodded her head quickly.

"That's not an answer, baby." I pulled her panties to the side, widening my eyes when I felt the moisture at her lips.

"Well, now. Are you going to answer me?" I swiped my fingers through her wetness and brought them to where our mouths remained nearly pressed together.

"Open your mouth, Melanie."

She parted her lips, and I slipped one wet finger in, watching her reaction as she tasted herself.

"More. Open more." I slipped the tips of the other two cream-coated fingers into her mouth and painted her lips with a mixture of her pussy juice and her saliva. When I pulled my fingers away, I immediately covered her entire mouth with a full kiss, licking and sucking, taking and consuming every inch of the inside and outside of her mouth with mine. When we parted, she looked as drunk as I felt from the experience.

"Dirty girl. I like it. You taste fantastic. I need more." I paused a beat as though I were formulating a plan. "Take off your dress."

She hesitated a moment with our gazes locked before turning around. "Can you unzip me, please?"

"It would be my pleasure."

She moved her ebony hair to one shoulder so I could easily access the zipper, but I leaned in and kissed her neck, continuing down to her shoulder and back instead. I gathered the fabric up around her waist and kneaded her ass while I kissed and nipped her skin, not able to get my fill of her creamy flesh.

"My zipper." She tapped on the metal tab with her index finger, which I quickly caught between my teeth.

"Oh!"

Her little yelp shot down through my dick, making my balls squeeze up closer to my body, encouraging me to make her cry out again. I pinched her ass a bit harder while biting her finger, confusing her senses as to which area felt more pain. And whether the pain actually hurt or felt good.

"Oliver!"

I released her finger and quickly pulled the zipper of her cocktail dress down to its limit. When I spread the fabric down her shoulders, the dress fell easily to the ground. I steadied her while she stepped from the garment, and then I quickly picked it up, smoothed it out, and laid it carefully over the back of the chair. I remembered that Jason Riley always took particular care with his ladies' clothes, so I wanted to make sure I impressed that upon her. She gave me a coy smile, and I knew it hadn't gone unnoticed. I had to remember this was a business I was building, and I would rely on recommendations for securing future clients.

My clothes were divested in record time. I laid them on the chair beside hers but not nearly as carefully. I didn't want to keep this woman waiting a second longer than necessary. Earlier, I had made sure I had condoms in my wallet, so I quickly slid one on. I wanted to be ready in case things went faster than I planned. I had a feeling Melanie hadn't been satisfied sexually in a long time, and I was worried when I got my mouth on her pussy, all bets would be off with taking it slow.

Melanie lay back on the bed, and I crawled up between her legs, scraping my nails lightly along her calves, up her thighs, and then spread her wider so I could settle between them for a feast.

"No. No. Just fuck me." She tugged on my shoulder while she whispered her plea. "Please. Just please. Put your cock in me." As if she had an inside track to my earlier thoughts, Melanie's begging tempted my resolve.

"Let me make it good for you, baby. Slow down. We have all night." I moved to rest between her thighs again, and she stopped me once more.

"You don't understand. It's been so long. I feel like I'm going to explode if you don't fuck me."

"Do you trust me?" Riley had major trust issues with everyone in his life, and I had no choice but to pull the book boyfriend card.

"I do." She had a look of desperation in her eyes, and I got the sense it had nothing to do with the story we were pretending to be a part of. "You just don't understand." She hesitated to say more. Then finally, "It's been so long since a man touched me. I mean really touched me."

"Then let me take care of you. Lie back and let me take care of everything. Your only job is to feel good."

She settled back into the pillows and closed her eyes.

"No, Melanie." I waited until she opened her eyes and looked directly at me. "Watch me."

Her eyes sprang open wider and she sat forward, but I gently pushed her back by her shoulder. "I said lie back. You don't follow instructions very well."

Grinning, I finally settled in between her thighs, kissing her velvety skin with lazy swipes of my tongue mixed in. In the pale light streaming in from the windows, I could see the goose bumps break out on her flesh.

"You're so responsive. So eager." Touching her could be habit-forming. So silky, so smooth.

"Put your mouth on me. Please. I'm begging you."

"Why the rush, sugar?" A weaker man would've been balls deep already.

"I need to feel you. Need to know if this is real." She raked her fingernails through my hair, igniting the nerve endings in my scalp.

"Oh, it's very real." I wanted to find the bastard who'd neglected this beautiful creature and given her this worrisome complex and beat the living shit out of him.

The next fifteen minutes were spent lavishing her pussy with attention. Minding her breathing and body's undulations, I discovered what she liked and what she *loved*. I took her right to the edge and then brought her back. Her frustrated cries throbbed through my cock in time with my heartbeat. When the knuckles of her clenched fists in the sheets were ghost white, I put the finishing moves on her and sent her spiraling into an epic orgasm. The wet spot beneath her quivering ass was my personal medal of honor.

"You doing okay?" I asked once her breathing settled down and she opened her eyes. The grin that spread across her lips gave me the answer I needed, but I wanted to hear the words too.

Her voice was husky and sexy from just having moaned through her pleasure. "Oh, I'm doing better than okay. I can't believe I'm going to admit this, but I don't remember the last time I had an orgasm."

I gathered her into my arms and held her there quietly while her breathing settled and her body relaxed again. My own mind had trouble centering while I took in every perfect detail of the woman. Her skin was silky and smooth as I ran my fingers back and forth across her shoulders before threading them through the long strands of her dark hair. It had been so long since I just lay with a woman in my arms and simply enjoyed the nuances of her femininity.

"Are you even listening to me?" Melanie tugged on my arm to get my attention.

"Huh? I'm so sorry. I was lost in my own thoughts." I kissed the top of her head.

She smiled. "I see that. Care to share?"

"It's probably not that interesting." Damn, her hair smelled good. Some sort of sexy herb, maybe lavender.

"I don't know." She raised one eyebrow and grinned. "You seem pretty creative."

"Is that right?" I liked where this was headed. Maybe I'd get to feel inside that sweet pussy after all.

She stretched up and kissed me, and I was all too happy to kiss her back. My cock, left unsatisfied, twitched immediately in response. She giggled in the middle of our kiss when my dick poked into her stomach.

"I think there's something that needs to be taken care of," Melanie whispered.

She wrapped her slender fingers around my shaft and squeezed. I let my eyes fall closed and flared my nostrils wide while inhaling deeper. Her musk flooded my senses and made my cock harder instantly.

"I can get on board with that plan. Scoot over here a little bit. You don't want to be in that wet spot." I moved farther toward the center of the bed so she would be more comfortable.

"Oh! Such a gentleman." She scooted beneath me, lying flat on her back.

I bit into her shoulder at the spot I had been kissing. "Let's not get carried away." I ran my hands across her breasts, thumbing her nipples as they peaked from the attention. "Your body is so responsive. How do you not have someone to enjoy this? I'd have my hands all over you all the time." I leaned down and sucked the flesh on the underside of one of her breasts between my lips, knowing the area was typically very sensitive.

"It wasn't always this way," she answered.

"I apologize. I shouldn't be asking personal questions." Making out was the best way to end this conversation and move on to better thoughts, like what those soft, plush lips would feel like wrapped around the head of my cock. I moved my hands over every peak and valley of her body again until I couldn't hold myself back any longer.

Her pussy was nice and slick from her orgasm and our make-out sesh. Fisting my erection, I ran the head through the moisture several times before lining up at her entrance. When I started to press forward, I met with more resistance than I expected, and I had to slow down so I wouldn't hurt her.

"I told you it's been a while." Her whispered voice tickled my neck.

"I know. I know. I'm sorry. You feel so good, Melanie. So good."

She spread her legs wider and lifted them higher so her calves were level with my shoulders. I took her cue and quickly ducked my shoulders under her legs and jacked her ass up off the bed. At that angle, I could drive deeper into her in one smooth motion. She cried out first in surprise and then ecstasy.

"Oh my God, Oliver!"

"I know, baby. Hold on. It's just getting good."

I slid in and out of her a few more times at a slow pace, concentrating on how her face twisted in pleasure when I bottomed out against her clit. I made sure to repeat the exact same motion every time. By about the fifth repetition, she was digging her fingernails into my forearms, chanting my name like I was a god on Mount Olympus.

"Can you come again?"

"Somehow, I think yes," she said in between pants.

"What do you mean *somehow*?" I said with a cocky grin.

"It's just never happened before. Twice in one night." The staccato delivery of her sentence made me chuckle.

"Well, then, tonight's your lucky night." With that I smacked against her clit with the pads of my fingers and then rubbed my thumb in firm circles on top of the overly sensitized button while I sped up the pace of my strokes.

Sweat was starting to form on my brow, and my balls felt like they were about to burst because they were so tight against my body.

"Melanie, I need to come—are you ready?" Now my disjointed speech matched hers.

"Yes! God, yes! So close! Just keep going. Keep doing what you're doing." If we had neighbors in the room next door, they had no doubt we were on the final leg of this relay.

A few more strokes and it was done for me. Warm semen filled the condom as I felt her channel constrict on my shaft. Her high-pitched wailing confirmed what I felt, and her incoherent words made me smile like a second-time Grand Prix winner.

We collapsed to the bed, and I rolled to her side so I wouldn't crush her beneath me. I snaked my arm around her waist and pulled her against me. Nothing beat postcoital cuddling in my book, but I could feel her instantly pulling away.

"Hey? What's wrong?" I was already talking to her naked back.

"Nothing. Nothing is wrong. That was fantastic." She twisted to peck me quickly. She got out of bed and gathered her clothing from where I had set it on the chair.

"Where are you going?"

"I have to leave. I said I'd only be out until midnight. It's already eleven."

I hadn't even thought of that. The possibility that she wouldn't want to spend the entire night together hadn't crossed my mind.

"Can I just leave the money here on the table? Is that okay? I know we talked about PayPal in our email, but I'd rather not have the paper trail, if that's okay? It could get awkward." She made a wrinkled face like she just ate something sour.

"Sure." I wrinkled my face in kind. Sour barely cut it.

She went into the bathroom and closed the door behind

her. I was left staring at the dark panel, expecting...what? Answers to run across the door like movie credits rolled across the screen after everyone got up and left the theater?

I felt so awkward. Usually I was the one trying to find my clothes and sneak out before the woman woke up. Instead, I wanted to pull the covers up and shield myself from the vulnerability I felt all of a sudden. Why was I acting like this? A quick look under the covers proved I still had a dick, even though I was acting like a total pussy. But I felt used. And cheap. And the worst part? This was my idea. The whole thing was my idea.

CHAPTER FIVE

It turned out twelve-hundred dollars made feeling like a bitch go away pretty quickly. My second date was with a woman named Lenor. She fancied a particular mafia boss character who was epic to impersonate. She texted me the next morning and asked if it would be okay if she gave my number to some of her friends in her tennis club. Apparently there were a lot of women around Los Angeles who were fed up with the dating scene, and she thought I could make them feel pretty special too. Even if for one night.

Unfortunately, the woman I really wanted to hear back from, Melanie, disappeared from my life as quickly as she had appeared.

Word of mouth turned out to be a way better marketing strategy than anything I could've come up with myself. By the end of the second week, I had been on four dates and had over five thousand dollars in cash hidden in a shoe box in my closet. Cash was the preferred method of payment by far. No bank records, no credit card receipts, no history. In other words—no proof.

Friday night came, and I purposefully scheduled my date for a little later in the evening so I could spend some time with Skye when she got home from work. I had a nice bottle of

Chardonnay chilling when she walked in the door, looking like she needed something stronger.

"Whoa, kiddo." I handed her a glass. "On second thought, maybe I should just get you the bottle."

"That's not a bad idea after the day I've had." She kicked off her pumps and took the glass I offered.

"What's going on? Is it something you can talk about?"

"You know I tell you everything. Even the stuff I'm not supposed to. I just don't want to get into it again. Let's just say I will be so happy when this election is over. You think Hardin is a rat?" A long pause while she drained half the glass. "The other guy the mayor is considering? Michaelson? He makes Hardin look like a Boy Scout. This race is getting so dirty. Soon they're going to be digging stuff up on me."

Chardonnay went down the wrong pipe in my throat, and I sputtered and choked. As selfish as it was, my best friend vented about her day, and all I could think about was myself. If anyone looked into Skye's background, they would discover things about me too. She and I had been inseparable for at least eight years. I would never forgive myself if my poor judgment hurt her career. In any way at all. And, if I was being completely honest with myself, if I had any shred of hope of saving my modeling career, all bets would be off if the press caught wind that the once unstoppable Oliver Connely had resorted to selling himself to horny housewives in order to pay the rent.

"You okay, Ollie? You look like you've seen a ghost." She was literally the only person who got to call me that name. My heart warmed while color hopefully returned to my face.

I drained my glass and quickly refilled it. I topped hers off too while I had the bottle in my hand. This was going to be one of the worst conversations we had ever had, and some liquid fortitude would hopefully make it easier. If things were really heating up at her office, I had to tell her about my current moneymaking activities before someone else did it for me. Maybe if I showed her the cash I had on hand, she would be dazzled by the Benjis and the *how* wouldn't be as important as the *how much*.

Oh Christ. Who was I kidding? This was Skye Delaney we were talking about. My best friend of all time. Dana-Do-Right. Captain Morality. Savior of all things that were just and fair. Able to list the Bill of Rights—by memory—at age ten. If she hadn't majored in constitutional law, she would've been a perfect choice for the next civil rights movement figurehead.

Regardless, I needed to man up and tell her what I was up to.

"Where are you going?" she asked when I suddenly sprang up and headed toward my room.

"One sec. I need to show you something." I came back with the huge wad of cash I had stashed in my closet. Roughly five thousand dollars. Mostly hundreds, some twenties, and a few lowly tens on the bottom from when I had to pay various cab drivers.

"Jesus, Oliver. Why do you have all that cash lying around? Better question, where did all that cash come from?" She volleyed her stare from the pile of money now fanned out on the breakfast bar to me and then back again while waiting for me to explain.

"I've been working a new job. I wanted to pay you back for my half of the rent from last month and pay the entire rent myself this month. To make up for all the times you covered for me." Hopefully the do-right bullshit worked for a guy like me too.

"You know that isn't necessary." She leaned over and eyed the stack of bills from a different angle. "And by the looks of it, that will more than cover it. Since when does Harrison pay you in cash?"

"This didn't come from modeling." No sense beating around the bush.

"Okaaaayyy. Are you going to make me guess what's going on here, or are you just going to tell me?"

This was it. My turn at bat. Steppin' up to the plate. Called up to the big show...

"I've been doing some..." Shit, the expectant look on her face made spilling the beans so much harder than I'd estimated. "I don't really know how to explain it."

"Start from the beginning. That usually works." Her patience was already wearing thin. Maybe now wasn't the best time to tell her.

No. It was now or never. Her career could be in jeopardy because of me if someone else found out before I told her. Maybe a personal example—something she could relate to— would help.

"You know those books you like to read? With the hot guys on the covers? Looking all beefy and brooding? Typically shirtless?"

She laughed but shook her head. "Yeah, I guess. Oh my

God, Oliver! Did you do a cover shoot? For who? Do I know the author? Who is it? Wow, so exciting. Wait, no...you said you didn't get this cash modeling."

Damn it, why didn't I think of that angle? She was actually excited about the prospect. What did those gigs pay?

When I held up my hand so I could get a word in, she stopped long enough to let me explain. "So, one day, I was at the pool—it was the first day I met Janine, actually. She was talking with a bunch of her friends, and they were going on and on about a book they were reading. But mostly they were talking about the main character. They were calling the dude their book boyfriend. It was the day I lost the Lagerfeld job."

"Damn Lagerfeld," we both mumbled under our breaths in unison while draining our glasses a second time.

I shook my head to get back to the real issue. "I'm serious."

"I know you are. So am I. I hate that freak."

"Anyway, the women were going crazy about this guy, how they all would love to get busy with him and so on. And it gave me an idea." I was getting amped up all over again, just like I did the day I thought of this idea. My voice gained volume, and I stood up from the barstool and started to pace, my animation adding wattage to the conversation.

"Oh God, Oliver." She buried her face in her hands. "I'm not sure I want to hear this. Thinking of Janine getting busy with anyone kind of squeebs me out, you know? Wait. Oh no. Oliver. Oliver...what are you saying? What are you doing with those women?" She peeked out between her fingers and squeaked. "Oliver? Did you sleep with Janine for money?"

"Let me explain." I quickly laid out the original idea, how

I placed the ad online, booked a week of dates in the span of one hour, and what was really going on when she found me on the floor with Janine that evening after work. I spoke quickly, trying to explain why the idea was a great one, feeling like I was on trial and also feeling like I was failing miserably at convincing her to see things my way.

"I'm making women happy, Skye. I would think you'd be proud of me for that. There aren't enough nights in the week to answer all the requests."

"Proud?" Skye was staring at me in disbelief. "You think I'd be proud you're whoring yourself out to desperate housewives?"

I looked at her incredulously. I leaned a hip against the back of the sofa and thought about what she was saying. "Well, not really. No. I don't see it that way at all, actually."

"Which part do I have wrong?" she snapped.

"For starters, I wouldn't say any of these women have been desperate. Not one." I dug my bare toes in and out of the weave of the carpet, trying to think of a better way to explain what I'd been doing for the past week.

"Oh my God, Oliver! Do you hear yourself?" Skye's voice was close to a screech.

"Don't be upset. I mean, Skye. Look at the money I'm making." I scooped up the money off the counter and fanned the cash out in front of her again.

"You're a prostitute! Oliver, for fuck's sake! A hooker! Really? You do know that is illegal in the state of California? You *know* that, right? You could be arrested. *Prison*, Oliver. Can you imagine what happens to a guy who looks like *you* in fucking prison?" Her face was beet red by the end of her diatribe, and spittle had collected at the corners of her mouth. There was a solid chance I'd never seen her that mad.

I leveled my voice, hoping hers would instinctively mirror mine. "Skye, you need to calm down. You aren't thinking about this rationally."

"Rationally? You mean there's a rational side to this? Oh...I can't wait to hear it."

"I'm not doing anything illegal. Nothing is agreed to ahead of time. I take a woman out on a date. That's it. If something else happens, that's something that just happens." Shrugging, I implied it was no big deal. "It's not what they are looking for in the beginning. It's not what the advertisement is for or even suggests. Believe me—I thought of everything." I couldn't help but still feel proud of the idea from a business standpoint. It was solid, and I was making money hand over fist. There was no denying it when I stood there with a wad of cash the size of a baseball.

"Everything? Really? Did you think of what this would do to me, Oliver? If the wrong person found out? No, wait. Let me rephrase that. *When* the wrong person finds out? Because they always find out, Oliver. *Always*. This was the most selfish, idiotic, thoughtless, reckless thing I think you've ever done." She chuckled sardonically. "And we both know you've pulled some doozies. I don't think I'll ever be able to forgive you for this one, my friend."

"But the money," I protested again. How did I get it so wrong? I thought she would be happy. At least once the shock of it all wore off.

"It's not always about money, Oliver." She shook her head in what I assumed was disappointment—or disgust. Could've gone either way at that point.

Anger finally broke through my calm. Her judgmental grimace transported me back to being reprimanded by my father, and I lashed out. "You have no idea what it's been doing to me! Not being able to pay my own fucking rent! I was a household name. People recognized me when I walked down the street, Skye. Now? Now, I'm nothing!"

"No. Now you're a prostitute. You can add that to your resume. Proud moment right there." She turned and started toward her room, only getting about two feet before swinging back with mock enthusiasm. "Hey! I have an idea! We should call your dad. He'd love to hear this. I can hear the pride in his voice now. Don't you think?" The venom in her voice was something I hadn't heard from her before. It made her unrecognizable.

"Wow." I swallowed hard. How could she hit so far below the belt? "Just—wow, Skye. That was low. Even for a bitch like you." I picked up the pile of cash and walked in the opposite direction toward my own room. I paused when I got through the door. The urge to slam it was so strong—but I chose to close it with extra gentle care instead. The effect was better. Our relationship had just suffered a critical hit, and the moment deserved a somber lone bugle calling "Taps," not a blazing horn ensemble's take on "God Save the Queen."

CHAPTER SIX

For the next two weeks, we managed to avoid each other like oil and water. When Skye came home, I was already gone. If I didn't have a date, I called up a buddy and went out to a bar or club. Anything to get out of the house. When I came home, she was already asleep. When I got up, she was already off to work. Our coexistence became more of an avoidance than a cohabitation. A dance where we carefully passed, like a car stuck in traffic on the 101 in rush hour and the motorcyclist who insisted on lane splitting to get through it. She squeezed by while I cringed and prayed we didn't collide.

But for some reason, my heart felt like it had already been in an accident when I thought about my best friend. I had hurt her, and I knew her well enough to know she didn't dole out forgiveness easily. I'd be lucky if we ever managed to repair our friendship. Deep down I knew I was risking alienating her with my business idea in general. It probably spoke volumes as to why she wasn't the one I went to for help rather than Janine, a neighbor I had just met. At the same time, I truly thought she'd come around when she saw how much money I was making. Maybe I didn't know her as well as I thought I did. I had never seen that venomous side of her that dealt the final blow in our argument. And for that, I was grateful. That was a part of

Skye Delaney I'd be glad to never see again.

Over the past twenty-one days, I had been on dates with twelve different women as their for-hire imaginary book boyfriend. I had portrayed everything from a navy fighter pilot to a cattle ranch owner. I was a motorcycle club president one night and a vampire lord the next. Every date took an extensive amount of reading and learning to pick up the nuances of the character. Janine helped me constantly. She quizzed me about facts and details that were particular to each man and also helped run errands to get my date-night supplies in order. She never accepted the money I offered her for her help. She told me her reward was knowing she was helping women live out their fantasies, even if only in some small way. I made her swear to tell me if any of the women from the pool ever said anything about calling Book Boyfriend Inc., because it would be way too awkward, and I would have to decline the date.

At that point, I had declined a handful of requests. Reasons varied, but most were all in the general category of "Crazyville." I'm a pretty open-minded guy, but I have my boundaries. A few women requested dates or characters that I just wasn't comfortable portraying, so those were turned down as well.

Thursday arrived, and I checked my calendar to see who was scheduled for the night. The client had requested very little, just stating she was looking for a quiet evening out, with maybe a nice dinner and some adult conversation. She named a few books she enjoyed from a series I was already familiar with. In fact, the character was quickly becoming one of the most requested book boyfriends I had, and the very first character I had portrayed: Jason Riley. He was the modern-day Casanova, and women couldn't get enough of him. I probably summoned that character twice a week. Each time brought memories of Melanie's beautiful face and magical green eyes that I usually had to work out of my system with a hand job before I could think of getting anything else accomplished. If only I could see her again outside of my fantasies.

But women's loneliness in general spoke volumes about the state of modern-day relationships. It was sad that this was what women requested, what they were willing to pay for. Not sex. Not some hot, crazy romp in a BDSM dungeon or to have her womanly virtues pillaged and plundered by a pirate captain and his crew. Just a quiet night together, maybe a nice meal. Even that wasn't a requirement. Most of my clients wanted good conversation and quality time. Women were lacking connection. Over and over again, that's what I was being told. They wanted to feel important in their partner's life. They wanted to feel like they mattered. That if the earth swallowed them up one day, their significant other would notice for reasons other than dinner wasn't waiting on the table or the laundry was piling up.

My own parents came to mind. I wondered if given the opportunity to date the Book Boyfriend, no strings attached, would my mother grab the brass ring? Hell, some of the women I had taken out had thriving careers outside the home. They were successful, smart, independent women. They had a lot going for them—all of them, regardless of profession. They just didn't have the one thing their hearts needed—attention.

All of the experience I was gleaning from this new job was going to serve me well if I ever decided to settle down. I would never leave my partner feeling neglected like so many others did. I suppose they never intended to do it. Things just transform over time: people change, become wrapped up in their jobs, grow complacent in their relationships, lazy in the nurturing and nourishment of their loved one's hearts and souls.

I made reservations at a quiet restaurant in the Wilshire District. It was a beautiful part of town, and there were a lot of upscale hotels nearby if things took a turn in that direction. But again, the large majority of the dates I had been on ended with a warm embrace, maybe a tender kiss, and I always insisted on a promise to make their own happiness a bigger priority in their daily routine.

Since most of the women who were seeking dates were from higher income brackets and used to posher accommodations, I always found restaurants in upscale areas. General life experience had taught me that any place with a higher price tag would be more discreet if the need arose. The expenses of the evening came off my bottom line, so I tried to keep costs within reason while still treating the lady to the type of evening she was accustomed to.

The Kimpton Hotel sat on the main drag in the neighborhood, so it was easy to find and parking was on-site. While checking my hair and outfit one last time in the mirrored walls of the elevator, the climb to the rooftop restaurant went quickly. I wore the book character's trademark sport coat and dark jeans, crisp white button-down shirt, two buttons open, showing just the right amount of chest hair. I had to laugh when I read those words in the novel the first time. Who decided what "just the right amount" of chest hair was, exactly?

When doing runway modeling, men were expected to have their chests waxed or clean-shaven for a show, unless the designer specified otherwise. If I shot a print ad, it was specified by the art director on the call sheet. So clearly, "just the right amount" of anything was subjective. In this case, I let nature do the talking. I wasn't a naturally hairy guy, but I had a small amount of hair on my chest. Hopefully my date considered it "just the right amount."

Panic set in. I couldn't remember her name. My date. I couldn't remember her name—no matter how hard I tried. The panic was making my memory worse. The only name that kept replaying in my head was that of the author of the book the character came from, and I was convinced that was made up, as most of them were. But I would've bet the entire fee for tonight's date that my lady's name wasn't Pepper.

Shit.

Penelope. Patricia. Petunia. Prinka. Prim. Porky. Pinky. Pepper.

Shit!

Polly? No way. That was a pet bird, not a woman. God, was it even with a P? Janine would know. I whipped out my phone to send her a text when I heard my name softly spoken from behind. Well, my character's name. I took a few seconds to send the text before turning to find one of the most breathtaking women I'd ever laid my eyes on standing a few feet away at the entrance to the bar area of the restaurant. It was Melanie, the woman I had my very first date with, and honestly, who I couldn't stop thinking of since. But why wasn't that the name she gave on this application? If I had seen Melanie on the calendar today, I would have definitely remembered. I should've waited for Janine's response. I should've saved myself the embarrassment of having to admit I couldn't remember her name. But my feet decided they needed to move toward her before some other guy, clearly much smarter than me, moved in on my turf.

Yes, I just said *my*.

She wasn't just beautiful; she was radiant. Literally, glowing with beauty I'd never seen before. Even more beautiful than my memory served. Something so untouchable and magnificent emanated from her, and every man in the room felt it too. It was as though someone followed her around with a spotlight, traveling just before her to provide the best personal lighting she could have at all times. Just the right setup to capture her perfect angles and curves, the heavenly way her hair cascaded down over her shoulders and flowed down to the middle of her back in soft curls.

Sssscccccrrrrrreeeeeeccccchhhh.

Hit the brakes, dude. What the hell was going on in my head? That was some serious pussy talk if I'd ever heard it, and it was coming out of my own brain. If I wasn't standing in front of one of earth's very own angels and wouldn't be risking making a royal fool of myself, I'd kick my own ass. The vibration of my phone brought me back to reality, and thank God for Janine, saving my hide again with the woman's name— although, as suspected, it wasn't Melanie. Maybe this was all part of the role-play she was looking for tonight. Whatever the game, I'd play along. Anything for the chance to spend another night with her.

"You must be Bailey?" I stepped in to offer my hand in introduction, but she backed away, holding her hand up in denial.

"No, I'm sorry. You have the wrong person." She turned and moved toward the bar to order a drink, and the disappointment and failure I felt took me right back to the moment Harrison told me about the damn Lagerfeld contract. *Bastard.*

I took a seat a few spots down at the bar and ordered an iced tea. I had a strict policy of no drinking on hired dates for several reasons. I didn't want to give the client the wrong impression; I definitely didn't want to be accused of something and have a fuzzy recollection of what actually happened the next day; and I certainly didn't want to have any sort of performance issues from too much alcohol if the date ended with a roll in the hay.

A quick decision had me texting Janine again to see if I'd gotten a profile pic with this client's application. She had started keeping physical files in her home office after the second week of the operation, seeing how successful things were becoming. When Skye had pointed out how my entrepreneurial endeavor could affect her career if discovered by the wrong person, I felt even better the records were being kept away from our condo.

Janine's responses were always quick, and she didn't let me down, other than to say there wasn't a picture in the file. She didn't waste the opportunity to remind me all the files were scanned and available via Dropbox, which she had taken a great deal of time showing me how to access just that afternoon.

Sometimes her implied "idiot" on the end of every comment rubbed me the wrong way. And maybe she didn't really mean it that way when she said things, but it could easily be taken that way. Like...every time. Maybe it was my own insecurity getting the better of me, and it was my own fault for letting her get away with it in the first place. I made a mental note to have a sit-down with Janine in the morning and set some ground rules about who was working for whom.

Regardless of what "Bailey" or "Melanie" or whatever name she was going by this evening had said, I still had the distinct feeling she was my date for the evening. And, for whatever reason, she wasn't ready to kick off the party. So I figured I'd just sit back and wait her out. If she was having second thoughts, I'd let her go at her own pace. It definitely wasn't a hardship to just sit and look at her, as most of the unattached men in the place were doing. What set me above the pack? The memories of what it felt like to be between those sexy legs. Or what her cries sounded like when she came, while I pounded into her over and over.

And why did that raise every hair on the back of my neck? Pretty ridiculous to feel possessive of someone who already belonged to someone else and was out catting around on them with you, wasn't it? But at least she'd returned for seconds. That was keeping hope alive.

While we sat there nursing our drinks for the next half hour, we tried to be inconspicuous as we checked each other out. I had the pleasure of watching her turn down two other suitors who offered to buy her drinks, telling them that she was meeting someone else. My patience was running thin, though, watching her cross and uncross her legs in perfect ladylike manner. All the while, having ideas of very unladylike things I'd like to see her do with what was between those legs. As my cock swelled a bit more in my jeans, she chose that exact moment to swivel her barstool in my direction and give me the sexiest come-hither smile.

Apparently, the cat-and-mouse games were over.

Or just getting started, depending on what kind of games she really wanted to play tonight.

"I'm starving," she finally said when I got right up beside her.

"Yeah, I feel that." It felt like the temperature in the room had been turned up about fifteen degrees. "I made reservations. Hopefully they held them, because they were for forty-five minutes ago when we were supposed to first meet here."

"I changed them when I walked in. It shouldn't be a problem." She threw a ten-dollar bill on the bar top as a tip for the bartender and grabbed her small clutch purse before sliding off the stool. I held my hand out to assist her, and she placed her delicate fingers in mine. Energy surged through me the moment we touched. We both stopped and looked to our entwined hands and then to one another's faces.

"You felt that too?" I asked, having never felt energy like that before from just touching a woman's hand.

"Yes." She looked back to our hands, almost confused.

"You're not like the others." I knew I shouldn't have said it out loud. I wanted to lash myself for letting it slip out, but it was too late to recall the words. And it was the truth. And if that made me lame or weak, well then, so be it. Something was unique about my body's reaction to this woman. I didn't even know her last name yet—hell, I wasn't even sure what her first name really was—but I knew she was going to be very difficult to get out of my system.

A fact I was already willing to bet my life on.

Dinner was fantastic, the view of the city unobstructed by other buildings or even by weather. The heaters on the rooftop deck made it pleasant to be outside, even at the late hour, and we sat together on one side of the table to share the heat created by the miniature furnace. I made a mental note to tip the waiter extra for the setup, even if he didn't realize the benefits I would reap from the layout.

For the first time since I'd started Book Boyfriend Inc., the date was easy and natural. The book character was shed like a molted skin within the first ten minutes of our meal, and I talked about myself, my own modeling career, my childhood, and hopes for the future. I listened, completely enthralled, as she did the same. I found out her real name was Bailey, but she didn't divulge her last name. She explained she had a husband in public office, which of course came as a shock but probably shouldn't have.

"Hey..." She reached over and held my hand. We'd been experimenting with physical contact throughout the meal. A stray hand that lingered, a taste of each other's meal, an arm around a shoulder to keep warm. "What's going on? What did I say? Your whole demeanor just shifted."

"You really don't miss a trick, do you?" I smiled because it was meant as a compliment, and she understood that without me explaining. Meeting an intelligent woman on the current dating scene was like finding a four-leaf clover.

"Tell me. You can tell me anything. I'm an open book. You're an open book. That should be our deal." She nodded emphatically as if her proclamation made it so.

"I think that's a good deal to have." I couldn't help but agree. I was so tired of the game playing in this town.

"Pinky promise?" She offered her smallest finger for the traditional shake.

"Yes!" We twined our pinky fingers together, and I tugged her closer and took the opportunity to kiss her after we shook fingers. The moment was too perfect not to. Her sweet lips yielded to mine instantly, which told me she wanted the kiss as much as I did. Even though it wasn't overly crowded, I didn't want to create a scene in the middle of the restaurant, so I lingered briefly and then pulled back. When she opened her eyes, she looked dazed and sated. Having that effect on her did great things for my ego.

"That was nice. Unexpected but nice." Her commentary was adorable. I wasn't used to a woman being so open with her feelings.

"Well, good. I'm glad you approve." I couldn't help the grin that crept from corner to corner of my mouth. I could feel the exact moment the dimples appeared, having lived with them my entire life, and knew I'd be in for a comment next.

"My God, Oliver, you are a beautiful man. Seriously. The angels wept when you fell to earth." She shook her head as she spoke, in what I could only perceive as disbelief.

"So poetic." I kissed her knuckles to take the attention away from me. "And a little depressing."

She laughed, little silver bells tinkling. "Why is that depressing?"

"I don't know... Angels weeping? Babies falling? That doesn't sound sad to you? It's like the 'Rock-a-Bye Baby' lullaby. Who makes this stuff up?"

"Okay, okay. You have a point. And you've successfully changed the subject."

"*Moi?*" I held my hand over my heart with mock hurt.

"Oh, cut the innocent act. I'm sure you are anything but that. In fact, I have firsthand knowledge." She took a sip of her water before adding, "To some degree."

"Offended. Party of one." I raised my finger as if requesting the check from the waiter, who of course, immediately scurried over to our table. We both laughed but thought we'd put him to use while he was there.

"Can I get you something else, sir? A nightcap perhaps? Coffee?"

I deferred to Bailey, and she ordered a cup of black coffee, so I had the same. When the waiter hurried toward the kitchen again, she just looked to me expectantly until I realized she was still waiting for me to explain why my mood had changed so drastically when she mentioned her husband and his profession.

I let out a sigh, not really wanting to spoil such a lovely night with my naivety about her marital status or talk of my feud with Skye. But to be honest, I knew better. Why else would someone like Bailey be interested in a Book Boyfriend?

The same reason the married women at my condo's pool were. So I pretended to be unfazed by that and instead focused on the situation with Skye, which was actually starting to weigh on me. Bailey asked, after all, and it might feel good to get it off my chest.

"So, I have a roommate who's been my best friend for a long time. She's in the same line of work as your...husband. She doesn't hold office per se, but she would love to someday. She works like a dog and seems very underappreciated by her boss—from where I sit, at least."

"If she's in politics, she's going to have to learn how to stand up for herself. Otherwise, she'll never get an elected position. It's a very cutthroat circle," said Bailey. "People are downright vicious. Is she sure that she wants to be a part of that?" She fiddled with her napkin while waiting for me to answer.

"She wants it more than anything else. She has as long as I've known her. We had a terrible fight recently, and it's eating me up inside. I thought I didn't really care about it, but the longer it goes unresolved, the more it's bothering me." I sat back in my chair and put my napkin on the table so the waiter knew he could clear my plate.

"You should apologize to her." Bailey was matter-of-fact.

"I should? What if she was the one who was wrong? Which she was, I might add." We both smiled, knowing I would say that whether it was true or not.

"Well, in my experience, it takes two to tango. And typically, when you fall on the sword, it's that much easier for the other person to follow suit. Lead by example and all of that." She waved her slim, feminine hand in the air, making me smile broader.

"I'm serious."

"I know, and I think you might be on to something. I've been wanting to talk to her; I just don't know the right way to go about it."

"Do you two have a history?" Again, her to-the-point method warmed my heart rather than put me on the defensive. I really liked this woman.

"We've been friends for a long time. We went to UCLA together." I knew where she was going with the question, but I thought making her work for it a little bit would be more fun.

"No, I mean a *history*." She said the word with a certain sensationalistic lilt.

I leaned in closer and stage-whispered, "Do you mean did we fuck?"

She mocked my tone in reply. "Yes."

"No." I sat back in my chair, smiling. "In all seriousness. We haven't. Ever. It's never been like that for us. It's just not there. You know?"

"Sounds a lot like my marriage." Now her tone drifted into Snarkville.

And just when there was something to dig my teeth into about her, the waiter showed up with our coffee. He made such a show of pouring the two cups of joe that I wanted to push him out of the way and do it myself just so we could get back to our conversation.

"This is going to probably sound odd, but I can't remember the last time I enjoyed just sitting and talking to someone as much as I'm enjoying being here with you right now."

"Well, thank you very much, Mr. Oliver Connely. I think

I'd have to agree with you."

"You must meet a lot of fascinating people with your husband's line of work..."

"Not really. Politicians are only interested in two things." She held her fingers up as she ticked them off. "Themselves and what you can do for them. That's it. So, for a woman like me?" She shrugged. "I'm disposable. As long as I sit there, look pretty, and don't embarrass him, I'm doing my job."

"But it's your marriage. Calling it a job seems so...so..."

"Impersonal? Distant? Unaffectionate? Cold?" She supplied the words with little emotional inflection.

"Yeah, that's the one I think I was looking for."

"Cold?"

"Yeah." Funny how she zeroed in on the same one I had from the entire list she had given. Or maybe not funny at all.

"Why do you think I ended up looking at your ad?" She took a sip of her coffee, and I noticed a slight tremble in her hand. The first sign of emotion all night, outside our undeniable physical connection.

"I guess when you put it that way..." I didn't know what else to say.

"Please don't think me heartless, Oliver."

"I don't. I see your heart." I gathered her hand in mine while I talked. I just wanted to touch her. Be close to her. "Your vitality. Your spirit seems bigger than many I've met in the last several years, actually. I think it makes me sad more than anything, if I'm being honest."

"Sad? Why would you say something like that?" She pulled her hand away to point to herself while she spoke. "Do

I look like I'm longing for anything? Look at me. I have it all. Anything I want. It's mine."

She appreciated the matter-of-fact approach so much, I thought I'd reciprocate. "Again, I'll point out the obvious, then. You looked up my ad. Twice."

She stopped talking completely and sat back in her seat where she had been forward on its edge almost the entire night. Something about the posture made me feel like I had put her in her place. Like I had sent an errant child to the naughty corner.

And I felt like the world's biggest asshole for it.

"Well, I had a lovely time with you tonight, but I think I should get going. My husband may wonder where I've gotten off to." She placed her napkin carefully on the table and reached for her bag.

"Please don't go. I feel terrible right now. Our night was going so well, and I feel like I've ruined it." Panic set in. I really didn't want her to leave.

"No. It's fine. You spoke the truth. Sometimes it's harder to face than others. That's all. I can wear the mask all day, Oliver, but depending on the way the sun shines down, you can see through the cracks." She pushed back in her chair, not waiting for me to do the gentlemanly assist in the least.

"Can I walk you downstairs?" I sprang to my feet, nearly toppling my chair back as I did so.

"No, I'll be fine. They have a valet, so I won't be on the street alone. And it's not like this is a bad neighborhood." She smiled a practiced smile meant to reassure me.

When she reached for her purse, I put my hand on top of hers. I didn't want our evening to end. "Are you sure I can't talk you into staying?"

"Not tonight."

"Another night?" I sounded like a desperate teenager.

"I'll call you, okay?" Next she would say, "It's not you; it's me."

"I hope you will." I walked with her to the bank of elevators and delayed pushing the call button. Another couple came into the vestibule, and I pulled Bailey off to the side to let them call for the elevator ahead of us. At least it would give me a few more minutes with her.

She was a small woman when we stood side by side. At least a foot shorter than I was, and she was wearing a killer pair of heels.

"Your shoes are fantastic. Stuart Weitzman if I'm not mistaken?" I leaned far out to the side to get a full view of her sexy legs and the shoes all in one look.

"The man knows footwear and looks like a Roman statue? What is this world coming to?" Her lighthearted smile was back.

"The hazards of life as a fashion model, I suppose." I shrugged, solid with my manhood, regardless of my extensive knowledge of women's shoe designers.

"Do you think your career is really finished? I see even middle-aged men and women in ads all the time. COVERGIRL has a seventy-year-old 'it girl' as we speak!"

"True. And she's fabulous. But it just depends what the designers are looking for from one day to the next, you know? And I need to pay bills and eat *every* day. I wasn't smart in the beginning when I was working nonstop. I didn't save or spend wisely, and now I'm panicking because of it. Hopefully I can get some extra in the bank and take jobs when they come and be choosy again about the contracts I take." All complete truth.

"I can't imagine anyone turning you away." She looked directly into my eyes when she spoke, and I wasn't sure if she was still talking about modeling gigs.

"Well, there are a lot of good-looking people running around this city." I stepped in closer to her, backing her up against the wall. "Can I kiss you again?"

"I was hoping you would. I've had coffee, though. Sorry." She put her fingers up to her lips, as if reconsidering her answer.

"So have I. Neither of us will even notice." We smiled as I moved closer, reaching under her hair with my fingers to cradle her head in my palm while I meshed our mouths in a perfect kiss. I stroked my thumb along her jaw, feeling her flawless skin while I tasted her lips and pushed in deeper to sample her further. Little humming noises escaped her when I changed the pressure of my tongue or tilted my head in another direction, keeping her guessing and accommodating my desires. When we parted, we were both panting and glassy-eyed, oblivious to the other two couples who had congregated in the waiting area for the descending elevators.

Bailey covered her face as a quick blush settled in, so I shielded her from the others while she regained her composure. I wasn't sure if she was actually embarrassed to be seen kissing me or if it was more about possibly being seen in public with someone other than her husband.

I waited until I was sure I had her attention and mouthed an apology to her, and she quickly dismissed it, so I felt marginally better. There was so much about her I wanted to learn and become familiar with. I was so scared I wasn't going to get a chance.

For the second time, the one woman I wanted to continue holding through to the next morning was the one who couldn't seem to get to her car fast enough. Watching her speed off in her adorable little two-seater convertible nearly gutted me. How the hell had I fallen for a woman over one date? Fine... two.

Maybe it was the shit with Skye that had me so off-kilter. I rode home thinking of ways to approach her. Maybe I'd get up early and have breakfast waiting for her before work. She never could say no to bacon. At least it would be a peace offering, a place to start mending our friendship.

From there I could try to get a handle on what was going on in my head and heart with Bailey. She was married and unavailable, so I shouldn't even be thinking about her. Not to mention, I had an entire month's worth of dates lined up with other women. Since that was my only source of income currently, I wouldn't be giving up that gig anytime soon either. So really, neither of us were in a position to get involved in anything beyond casual dating.

I needed to put the idea of Bailey up on a shelf for another time, when everything was clearer.

Ha! If only matters of the heart worked that way.

CHAPTER SEVEN

The water shut off just as I pulled the bacon from the oven. My mom taught me to make the greasy pork goodness that way, as it made much less of a mess than on the stove. I smiled, thinking of my mom and wondering what she was doing this morning. I'd have to give her a call later. It had been weeks since we talked, and I felt like shit when I realized it was probably more like months. I flipped the pancakes on the griddle, watching the fluffy pillows rise as the wet batter sizzled on the hot surface. I had all of Skye's favorites ready for her.

As if following a director's stage cue, her bedroom door opened and my roommate came out wrapped tightly in her fluffy white hotel robe, towel piled high on her head to keep her wet hair under some sort of control.

"Oh." She pulled up short when she saw me standing in the kitchen. "Well. Good morning." She couldn't even meet my eyes when she spoke, and it broke my heart that I let our relationship go to this extreme over something so silly.

"I'm just going to get some coffee. Damn, Oliver. That smells so good. Is that bacon?" She looked under the lid of the stovetop frying pan where the bacon was being kept warm.

"Can you spare a few minutes this morning? I was hoping we could have breakfast together." The best way to this girl's heart was her stomach. I knew it as sure as I knew my own name.

"You made all of this for me?" Finally, she looked me in the eye.

"Well, who did you think it was for?" This time I was the chicken, though, looking away, busying myself with the pancakes.

"I figured you had a guest."

"No, it's just us. And I know how much you love bacon."

"Mmmmm, I do love bacon." She grabbed a piece before I could swat her hand away and then went for a mug in the cabinet. "Do you want some coffee?"

"I could use a top off. Thank you." I handed her my cup from where it was sitting near the stove.

"Take a seat. Pancakes are coming up."

She walked around to the other side of the breakfast bar, clearing some space for me to move around our small condo-sized kitchen. "Oh, pancakes too? Wow. What's the occasion?" She dropped her spoon onto the bar. "Oh no. Are you moving out? Are you leaving me? I mean, I know we had that argument. I know I was awful. I'm so sorry, Ollie. Please don't leave me, though. Not over something like that."

"I'm not leaving, Skye. And I'm the one who should apologize to you. I didn't take your feelings into consideration when I started this." I put the plate of pancakes between us and sat down. "I don't even know what to call it. This venture? I guess we should've talked first."

She turned on her stool to look at me directly. "You think? I mean, it's prostitution, Oliver."

"Hey. Are we going to start again?" I set my fork down, two pancakes still stabbed through the center.

"No. No, you're right." She grabbed my hands in hers and squeezed. "I'm sorry. But I do think we need to talk about what you're up to. Maybe we should set up some ground rules or something. Like, I don't know...you can't bring random women here all the time to fuck for money?" She winced, letting go of my hands when the harshness of her words sank in.

"I wouldn't do that. And I told you, Skye, or I tried telling you, I'm not sleeping with them. Or not *all* of them. And I'm not setting up the dates with the express purpose of sleeping with them. Most of these women just want companionship. But we don't need to get into all of that. I just couldn't stand going another day with you mad at me. It's been eating me up inside." I layered butter and syrup on the stack of steaming goodness on my plate and went to dig in. After my mouth was full, Skye decided to hit me with the feels.

"You are the best friend a person could ever hope to have, Oliver. Do you know that?" She slid off the barstool at our little breakfast bar and came over to hug me. I stood up and lifted her off her feet in a giant brother bear hug that made her squeal until I returned both feet to the ground.

"I feel like I need to make this up to you. I swear I didn't think what I was doing would impact you in any way. Actually, I didn't think of you at all. And that's the worst part. It was selfish, and I didn't even realize it was, and that really scares me. Am I that incapable of coexisting with another human being? You know how much I love you. And I didn't even think of you. I just thought of myself and how this would get me out of the rut I was in."

We sat back down, but my breakfast food had lost its appeal. Skye, on the other hand, dug in to the pile of bacon on her plate.

"You need to lighten up, honey. As usual, you're being way too hard on yourself."

"It's just that I've been thinking about this a lot, and I know I screwed up. I've screwed up a lot of things, frankly."

"Have you been talking to your folks?"

"No, I'm serious." I appreciated her wanting to brush this off as one of my typical post-phone-call-home self-flagellations, but this one was all on me.

"So am I. You're not a screw-up, Oliver. You have so much to be proud of." She stroked my back while she complimented me. For some reason, it made me feel worse—like a child.

"Well, I did—I should have. I should have more to show for how hard I've worked. But I also should've listened. To them, and to you, and everyone else who tried to tell me that being so careless with my spending was going to catch up with me eventually. But hey, I was too smart for everyone, right? I was the guy who had it all figured out. Well, now the joke's on me. Now I'm the guy who can't even pay his rent."

"I can only fan your flames for so long here, my friend." Her reluctant comment halted my pity party.

"I know, I know. And that's not what I'm expecting from you. Really, it's not. This wasn't meant to be a pity party. It was meant to be me apologizing to you and really making a commitment to get better at this whole 'adulting' thing."

She looked at me sideways while taking a bite of her pancakes.

"What?" I hated that look more than any of her others.

"No, *you* what?" She paused a minute while I sat silent, having nothing more to add. And then abruptly said, "Exactly."

"I hate when you do that," I said with utter frustration.

"Do what?" Now she feigned innocence.

"Have an argument with yourself." I felt like I was stating the obvious.

"I'm not having an argument with myself, Oliver." And judging by her tone, she felt the exact same way about her point.

"Basically, you are." This would not be the hill I died on.

"Nooooo." She drew out the vowel sound in the word, either to make a point or be extra annoying; the jury was still out on which. "It's just my Grandma Lilian had a saying: Guilty minds need no accusers."

"What the hell is that supposed to mean?" Yep...extra annoying.

"Exactly what it sounds like. Think about it."

I mulled the words over in my head. She was hinting at the idea if you let someone stew in their own guilt long enough, they incriminated themselves with their behavior. I guess she was also implying, then, that by me insisting I wasn't looking for a pity party from her all the time that I was in fact driving the waaambulance right into the town square myself.

Fine.

Guilty as charged.

"Goddamnit, Skye. Why are you always right?"

"I'm not always right, Ollie."

I gave her the best imitation of her "Oh really" look I

could muster, and she burst out laughing, cutting through the tension that had built up in the room.

"Okay, I'm right a heck of a lot of the time. There, I said it."

"And really super humble about it too."

Suddenly she sobered. "Do you know what?"

"Hmmm?" I had just stuffed the last forkful of my breakfast into my mouth when she asked the question, so that was the best she was going to get in the way of an answer.

"I love you. With all of my heart. I know you have your reasons for doing what you're doing. I just think you're better than this. I think there's more waiting out there for you and you need to figure out what that is and not settle for entertaining Mrs. Robinsons day in and day out to make a quick buck."

"It's just until I get back on my feet. I've already saved a bunch."

"That's great." But she didn't look impressed, and her tone wasn't genuine either, so I felt like I needed to defend myself again.

"Really, I've come up with a long-range plan, with goals and everything. I have no intention of dating lonely women for the rest of my life. I just needed a way to make money so I don't feel like a leech. I can't handle becoming all the things my old man said I would."

"Is that what this is all about? I mean, when all is said and done, is that what this is, Oll? A good ole-fashioned Daddy issue?"

I shrugged. "Not completely, but a large part, yeah, I guess it is. He really did a number on me, Skye. I don't think you understand."

"Actually, I do. I just wish there were some way I could get through to you that you don't need to believe those things about yourself. No one thinks them, and you're putting yourself at risk for no reason."

"And you," I said quietly but knew she heard me.

"What?"

"I'm putting you at risk. And I feel horrible about that."

"It's not that bad. I'm sure I overreacted. No one even cares about me, Ollie. I was being dramatic and self-important. Forget all that nonsense, okay?"

"I won't. I'm going to take extra care to make sure I don't compromise your integrity with my behavior. I would never forgive myself. I know how hard you've worked to climb the steps at city hall. I know how much it all means to you."

"Well, maybe it shouldn't. Maybe I'm putting my energy in the wrong place."

"What do you mean? You love that shit." It was so rare to hear Skye question her decisions, let alone her life's path.

"Do I?"

"Whoa. What's going on? Who are you, and what have you done with Skye Delaney?"

"Hey, I get to have an identity crisis too once in a while, don't I?" She drew in the syrup left behind on her plate with the tines of her fork.

"You get to do whatever you want. You're the level-headed one around here."

"Let's not get carried away now. But if I don't get ready for work, I'm going to be in the line at the Unemployment Office tomorrow morning. Hardin would love to have a reason to give me the boot."

"He wouldn't know what to do without you. He'd be so lost, it would be sad and hilarious all at the same time."

"True. But it's not a theory I'm willing to test. Thank you for the amazing and greasy start to my day. I'm so glad we talked." She slid off her stool and started clearing her plate.

"Just leave it. I'll clean up. Go so you're not late." I batted her hands away from the dirty dishes.

"Are you sure? You did all the cooking. I should do the cleanup."

"Yeah, but this is a special day. It's part of the apology package." We both knew she sucked at cleaning up too. It was a little game we played: she offered, I refused, and so it went.

"Oh! I think I like the apology package, then! Because just between you and me, I hate cleaning up as much as I hate cooking."

"I know, baby. But we can't let you be too much of a princess, or no one will ever want you." I smacked her on the ass just before she moved out of reach.

She stuck her tongue out and skipped off toward her room. At the last moment, with her hand resting on the handle of her bedroom door, she turned back toward me.

"Oh my God! Oliver, I almost forgot! Don't forget the Auxiliary Charity Ball for the hospital is in two weeks and you promised to be my date."

"Oh shit! I'm so glad you reminded me. I better make sure my tux is here. I think it may still be at the cleaners."

"Nope, I picked it up yesterday. It's in your closet—right on the end. I took it out of the bag so it could breathe."

"You are the perfect woman, Skye Delaney. I've said it before, I'll say it again. Why you haven't let some man sweep you off your feet is beyond me."

"Oh please! As I've told *you* before, I don't need a man to ride in here on his white horse and save me. Who has time for all that bullshit anyway? And who says I wouldn't be doing the saving? Hmmm?"

"Go. To. Work, Wonder Woman."

While I cleaned up the dishes, Skye got ready in record-breaking time. I couldn't help but think to myself that she really would make an excellent wife. But she would be one hell of a ballbuster of a spouse too. I don't think a man alive could live up to her expectations and demands. She was a great roommate and the perfect best friend, but I knew for certain I hadn't come across a man yet who could go toe-to-toe with that woman and come out on top.

CHAPTER EIGHT

"I'm so glad you were able to make it tonight." I poured a glass of Chardonnay for Bailey, handed it to her, and then poured one for myself. She waited to take a sip until I had mine in hand.

"So am I," she said as she held her glass up to mine in a toast offering.

We clinked glasses together and enjoyed a sip, although I couldn't take my eyes off her long enough to hear another word she said along with it. She moved around the living space of our condo, looking at the paintings Skye had hung and a few of the portfolio pictures I had around the house. When she caught me watching her looking at a particular shot a little longer than the others, she turned a stunning shade of fuchsia that made her cheekbones even more pronounced.

"I know I shouldn't say this...but I've been thinking about you a lot." I crowded into her personal space while telling her my confession.

"Why is that something you shouldn't say?" She looked up at me, our height difference more pronounced because we were both just wearing socks. Skye's germaphobe rules for inside the house—no shoes.

"I don't know. Maybe it makes me look like I'm a sap or

something?" Or in way over my head?

Or a Stage-Five Clinger? Red alert! Red alert!

"A sap? I don't think I've heard that word in a really long time." She turned and went to sit on the sofa, putting distance between us again.

"I grew up in the Midwest. I probably can blame a lot on that. It's my go-to excuse for a lot of things, now that I think of it." I went for the boyish grin.

"I think it's charming."

Bingo!

Grabbing the popcorn off the breakfast bar, I went to join her on the sofa. "Then sap it is. But I still can't believe you've never seen *Spaceballs* before. It's a classic."

"No, Oliver." She let out a big sigh but was grinning. "Classics are things like *Gone with the Wind* and *A Streetcar Named Desire*. Not a Mel Brooks movie."

"I think you should reserve judgment until it's over. If you laugh at least twice, you can never dis Mel Brooks again."

"Fair enough. Pass the popcorn, though. If I'm going to endure a movie featuring John Candy dressed like a dog, I'm going to require salty snacks. Possibly chocolate."

I handed her the bowl of popcorn I made before she came over. "Deal!"

Skye was out for the night with her girlfriends from her old sorority. They usually got together a few times a year, and when they did, it was an all-night affair. I had gone out on a limb and invited Bailey over to watch a few movies and just chill at our place. By the grace of God, she'd said yes, and I was the happiest I had been all week.

Three dates as the Book Boyfriend in the past week had nearly sucked the life out of me. I wasn't sure how much longer I could keep it up. There was a friend of mine from the modeling circuit I was considering bringing into the fold to help take up some of the overflow. Word was spreading like wildfire about the service, and I just couldn't keep up with the demand. If I brought a second man into the mix, I could satisfy the client demand and also take a cut of what he brought in.

I never intended for the business to expand beyond a one-man operation, but suddenly it was something to consider. Skye would be the perfect person to run some ideas by, but I wasn't convinced she could remain objective. I'd already talked to Janine about it, and she thought the idea was fantastic. In fact, I'd had to push her out the door midsentence before Bailey arrived, fearing she'd still be plotting our world domination.

Spending the evening with Bailey cuddled on our sofa, watching movies from the eighties, was exactly what my head and heart needed. We laughed at all the ridiculous bits in the *Star Wars* spoof, and I think she enjoyed it more than she let on. In a fair, best two-out-of-three thumb wrestling match, Bailey won the right to pick the second movie. So we watched *Sixteen Candles*—a John Hughes flick from 1984 that every teenager from that era had seen at least twice.

"Are you crying?" I sat forward so I could get a better look at her beautiful, tear-streaked face.

She quickly swiped at her cheek with the back of her hand "No, I'm not crying. Don't be ridiculous!" A second swipe to the other cheek then.

"You were crying! This is over that Jake Ryan guy, admit

it!" I teased her about the handsome young character from the movie.

"I was not crying. And besides, every girl loves Jake Ryan. He's perfect. I mean, look! He's waiting for her. He's just standing there waiting for her." She looked back to the television wistfully. "Everyone else forgot. And he's there waiting. The Porsche doesn't hurt, let's be honest." Another tear slid down her cheek, and this time I wiped it away with my thumb.

"I don't think there's anything wrong with believing in love," I said quietly.

"Well, in real life there is. I'm not so sure such a thing really exists." She shrugged.

"Awww, don't be so cynical." I hugged her closer to my side as we snuggled on the sofa.

"Says the incarnation of Jake Ryan himself. And may I point out, I'm not being cynical. I'm being realistic. I'm an unhappily married woman lying in another man's arms. I'd say waxing poetic about love would be a bit hypocritical, wouldn't you?"

"I guess you're right. But I have to speak to your first point. I'm way better looking than that Ryan guy. I'm just saying." I gave her a playful wink so she knew I was teasing and didn't think I was really that conceited.

"I was thinking more about the born romantic inside of you being like Jake."

"Oh? You think it's romantic that I invited you over to make out on my couch?" I tried to give a wolfish waggle of my eyebrows, but her laughter convinced me I'd failed in looking sinister at all.

"Who said anything about making out?" She tried to feign offense.

"Well, we're definitely going to. It's a total given." I moved so I was positioned above her, pressing her back into the cushions of the sofa.

"How do you figure?" Her slender fingers sifted through my hair until her nails scraped my scalp, instantly igniting my nerve endings.

"I made popcorn and everything. It's totally a sure thing. And, since you got to choose a chick flick, I totally think second base is in order. At a minimum." I tugged on the zipper of her sweatshirt. She had shown up to my condo under the guise of having an appointment with her trainer, and I had a million thoughts of how to give her body a thorough workout as she lay beneath me.

Her laugh was so low and husky, it felt as if there were actual fingers strangling my dick. This relaxed, easy side of her was so enjoyable and carefree compared to the measured, sophisticated woman I had dinner with the other night at the Kimpton. While also very enchanting and pleasant, kicking back and watching movies at home showed an altogether different side of Bailey.

I couldn't wait any longer to kiss her. I'd been wanting to do so all night, and my restraint had met its limit. Since we weren't in public, I really had the chance to explore her this time. Her body was tight and toned. The swell of her ass fit perfectly in my palm as I caressed and kneaded her through the thin material of the yoga pants she wore. I turned my body so I could press more of her beneath me, settling between her legs with the bulk of my weight so I wouldn't crush her, simultaneously pressing my erection into the vee where her legs came together.

"Oh. Wow! That feels...urgent." She chuckled against my lips.

"I've been thinking about you a lot lately." I circled my hips against her mound another time to let her feel just how *urgent* things really were.

"Oh. Mmmm." She moaned. "I see. But I would think this occupation of yours would have a lot of other ladies around to ease your *urgencies* as well."

Thinking the statement was more of a fishing expedition, I wasn't sure how far to go in the way of explanation of what went on during most of the dates. What did I owe her, really? I was totally into her, but she was married, for starters, and had made it very clear she wasn't interested in being a thing beyond an occasional date. I half expected her to push me away at any second.

Kissing a path down her neck, I was careful not to leave a mark, even though I was overwhelmed with a desire to sink my teeth into her flesh. Some women just had the type of skin that begged you to bite or suck, and Bailey definitely did. Perfectly white, pale from every angle, as if never kissed by the sun's rays. I nibbled on her ear, and she moaned, lifting closer for more, and smiled.

"I could get used to you, Oliver. I think I like the way you move."

"You haven't seen me move, Bailey. Not yet anyway."

"Oh, you know what I mean, though. There are just things a woman can tell about a man."

Leaning back, I was tempted to break away completely to hear more of this theory. "Is that right?" I grinned, knowing I couldn't really keep away from her taste now that I was this close. I kissed down her neck and down into her cleavage, cupping her breasts roughly through her hoodie. Her praise was inspiring me to show her just how much I could please her. I licked her roughly, raking my fingers through her hair and tugging her head back when I had a handful of her tresses. Her moans made my cock swell thicker.

"Oliver. God. Yes, so good."

I covered her moans with an openmouthed kiss, coiling my tongue roughly with hers. Our breaths were hot and heavy, mixing as we panted against one another, the tempo of our make-out session increasing in an uneven pattern. When I yanked the zipper open on her sweatshirt, she stared up at me with glassy eyes. Chest heaving with labored breaths, her eyes closed.

"We need to settle down. This is getting intense." She pushed to sit up but couldn't really get far with me on top of her.

With timing worse than an alarm clock ringing in the middle of the best sex dream ever, her cell phone started playing "Hail to the Chief" from where she'd left it sitting on the end table near the sofa.

"I can imagine who that must be," I mumbled like a bratty teenager, unable to hide my pissy attitude about being interrupted. But seriously, "Hail to the Chief"? She had said he was in local politics, hadn't she?

"Hey there. Oh, I'm sorry. Who's this?" There was a pause, and Bailey sat forward, zipping her sweatshirt all the way up to her neck.

I listened to her greet her husband, dick deflating faster than if I had taken part in the New Year's traditional Polar Bear Plunge back home in Iowa. But after only a few more seconds, I began to realize something was wrong.

Very wrong.

Bailey hadn't said another word in the conversation but listened intently, nodding at various intervals as if the person on the other end of the phone line could see her. The normally pale skin I adored on her face had gone ghostly white.

Dropping to the sofa beside her, I waited to see what I could do to help or comfort her.

"I see. Where is he now?" She paused, presumably to let the person answer her question, and then continued. "Thank you. No. I know where that is. Yes. I'm leaving right now." She stood and then immediately sat back down again, bewildered and trembling. "No, I was with my trainer. I'll leave right now." She rose to her feet once more, this time patting her pockets looking for something. "Yes. Yes, thank you." She stopped again, turning away from me and swiping at her cheek like I had seen her do earlier when I teased her for crying while watching the movie. "Is he...is he..." Her voice, barely audible, cracked. "Is he alive?"

She pressed a button on her phone and tossed it into her purse after I handed it to her. I was smart enough to put the pieces together from what I heard of the conversation. Bailey looked at me, tears welling up in her eyes once more.

I held my arms open for her, and she quietly stepped into my embrace, sobbing against my chest while I stroked her hair. There wasn't a lot I could say. Her husband was either dead or clinging to life, and whatever had happened, it occurred while she was with me.

Finally, when she pulled back, I offered, "Why don't I drive you? I don't think you're in any shape to be behind the wheel. We don't need a second tragedy tonight."

"Okay. I think that's a good idea. Can you drive me in my car, though? I don't need reporters seeing me pull up in a strange car. They're already going to have a field day with this mess."

"Of course. We can even swap a few blocks away. You can drive the final stretch, and I can Uber back here."

"You wouldn't mind doing that?" Her green eyes had darkened with emotion.

"Not at all. I just want to be here for you. Can you tell me what's going on?" I didn't want to pry, but I wanted to know exactly what we were dealing with.

"I'll explain on the way. I need to get to the hospital, and I'm guessing we're about twenty minutes from Cedars?"

"That's fair. Plus, traffic shouldn't be bad at this hour." I took a quick peek at my watch to confirm the time after making the promising remark. "Let me just grab my phone and wallet, and we can go."

Bailey explained the situation while I drove us to Cedars. Her husband had been brought in after a 9-1-1 call was made from a hotel on the opposite side of the city from where she and her husband lived.

"Was he at an event this evening?" Maybe I sounded naïve, but I didn't want to assume the worst about a guy I didn't even know. After seeing the look she threw my way, I realized the only event he had been attending was a private party for two.

"Oooohhhh...I understand now... I'm sorry. I guess—"

"Why are you apologizing, Oliver? My husband hasn't been faithful for years. Maybe ever. It's not your sin to atone for." Bailey's tone was so matter-of-fact, it was disturbing. Out of place. I didn't know how to react, so I concentrated on driving, even though traffic was unusually light and her little sports car handled like a dream. The silence in the car thickened like the June morning coastal fog. If I said something at that point, it would have been even more awkward than if I had said something immediately after her cold remark about her husband's infidelity.

"Please don't judge me," she finally said. Although it was said quietly, it shattered the silence like a tiny tap to a windowpane that splintered the entire surface. I wanted to pull off the road and take her in my arms, comfort her not only for what she was enduring in the moment but for what she had tolerated for countless years.

"Judging you is the last thing on my mind, Bailey. I want to comfort you...I don't know—exact justice on your behalf— somehow take all the pain away."

"Pain? From him cheating?" She scoffed, and I immediately felt defensive. "Oliver. Be serious. I knew exactly what I was getting into when I married him. He always had his sights set on a career in politics. Even when we were at

Berkeley. That's all he could think about—dream about. And I was right there alongside him." Her voice drifted off to wistful midway through the speech.

"I was part of his big plan. The good wife. The perfect politician's wife. And unfortunately, I learned rather quickly, with power, came groupies." I could see her look in my direction from my peripheral vision while I drove. "It's not just for actors and musicians, you know. Young ladies—and young men—have no qualms about sleeping around to get what they want. And people in positions of influence, even in the local offices like my husband, are all too willing to oblige them. The thrill of their own importance goes to their head, and before you know it, they find themselves in a hotel room across town, having massive cardiac arrest while the flavor of the month keeps riding their Viagra-induced boner until they realize he's actually unconscious from a medical emergency and not the designer drug they both did just minutes before."

When Bailey finally finished talking, she sagged back into the contour of the seat and burst into tears, burying her face in her hands while her entire body trembled with emotion.

At the next street, I pulled over, put the car into park, and turned off the headlights but left the engine running. I unfastened my seat belt so I could turn fully toward Bailey in the passenger seat.

"Bailey." I stroked her hair while she cried, but she wouldn't look at me. I wanted to hold her in my arms, but the damn center console made it impossible. "I want to hold you so badly right now. Come here. Let me touch you at least... I feel so helpless sitting here watching you sob."

Finally, she came into my embrace the best she could and let me comfort her while she cried. I cooed and shushed her, not really knowing what else to do while she let her emotions free. We sat there for a few short minutes before she abruptly pulled back and sat squarely in the passenger seat again, apparently deciding crying time was over.

"I'm sorry you had to see all of that." Her voice was hoarse with tears, but she cleared her throat a few times, banishing the nuisance evidence betraying her humanity.

"I'm not. I'm grateful you trusted me enough to share your emotions." I tried to keep my voice level, while inside I was furious watching what she was putting herself through.

"Who are you?" she murmured, shaking her head.

"Sorry?" She continued to baffle me.

"I mean what person, what guy even says something like that?"

Although it wasn't intended to be an insult, it was rubbing me as if it were. "I don't know? A real one? I know that was probably a rare moment. Especially based on the little bit you just shared with me, so I felt like thanking you for trusting me enough to open up in front of me was in order. I won't betray your confidence."

"Well, I appreciate that, Oliver. I really do. We need to go to the hospital, though. Hopefully he's still alive. They didn't sound hopeful when they called before." She pulled down the visor to check her makeup in the small light-up mirror on the back side.

"Okay. It's just a few more miles. Do you want to take it from here? This is a pretty quiet street. I doubt there are any reporters this far away from the hospital." As much as I hated to leave her, it was as good a time as any.

"You're probably right. Are you sure you'll be okay?" she asked, her voice concerned and strong once more.

I just gave her my best "be serious" look and got out of the driver's side of the car.

When we met at the back of the vehicle, I quickly took her in my arms and held her close. She felt so small and vulnerable in my arms, and I wished I could be with her at the hospital but understood why she needed to keep up appearances. I leaned down and pressed my lips to hers, wanting to part with the taste of her on my tongue. We meshed our mouths but then parted too quickly.

"Please let me know if I can do anything for you. Anything at all." I said the words against her hair, breathing in her scent to memorize everything I could about her.

"I will. I'll call you when I can. It may be a while, though. You understand?" She looked up to me, eyes so emerald in the light from the streetlamps.

"Yeah. Sure. I get it. I'll be thinking about you." Really, what more could I say?

"Okay. Thanks, Oliver." She kissed me softly, one last time.

"Bye, Bailey. Take care of yourself."

"You do the same."

With that, she got back in her little car, the same one I remembered watching her drive away from the Kimpton on the second night we met, and sped off toward Cedars-Sinai. I couldn't help but wonder what sort of a relationship could really be built with a woman who I routinely watched drive away. The bone-deep fear that it would be the last time I'd ever see her was probably answer enough.

Just when I thought I'd found a woman I could really enjoy spending time with, fate played its cruel symphony from an out-of-tune orchestra.

A show for which I would *not* stand and demand an encore.

CHAPTER NINE

The weekend went by slowly. I tried to stay busy with organizing my business plan for Book Boyfriend Inc. I did research online regarding business license requirements, fictitious business name filings, becoming a limited liability corporation versus incorporating fully, and other such exciting things.

While the smaller details made my eyes roll back in my head, I was really energized by the prospect of taking the idea to the next level and becoming a legitimate business. The growing popularity of "investment dating" was going to be where I would capitalize the most. While services commonly focused on men as the investors, women were being ignored. Until now, at least. There was a gap in the market, and I had every intention of filling it. I found a few company sites I really admired. Their business models looked like something I could emulate and their philosophies lined up with mine, so I bookmarked those to research more and possibly join to see how they ran from the inside out. However, researching dating services opened a whole other can of worms I didn't expect. The gray area between dating service and prostitution wasn't as wide as I had originally thought. No wonder Skye was so angry the first night I'd sprung the concept on her.

Speaking of my best friend, she still hadn't wandered in from her night with her girlfriends, and by that point, nearly thirty-six hours had passed. I checked in with her twice, and both times she said she was fine, just nursing a dreadful hangover at her college dorm roommate Laura's house. I resisted texting a jab about not being able to keep up with the kids anymore and moved down to Bailey's name on the screen instead.

She had texted twice throughout the night with brief updates. Her husband was not well, unstable and likely not going to survive the massive heart attack he'd had. She didn't want to go into any of the details of the actual incident that led up to the attack via text, and I respected that. I offered to bring her food or a change of clothes, but she said her assistant was already there with her and was handling everything, so at least I knew she was in good hands. I hadn't heard any more from her for about twelve hours. I checked the local news feed online and had the television on the local station with the sound muted, but as of that morning, there was nothing being reported on the news. It made me realize I didn't even know Bailey's last name, nor did I know much about her husband, other than he held a local office.

Maybe Skye would know. I sent her a quick message and hopped into the shower. It was already past noon, and I couldn't handle sitting inside any longer. Just as I was stepping out of the steamy glass stall, my cell phone rang from the vanity. When I saw Bailey's number, my heart leaped like a high schooler seeing his big crush in the hall between classes.

"Hey, beautiful. How are things?"

"Hi, Oliver. I hope I'm not calling at a bad time. I realize it's Sunday."

"What does that have to do with anything? And I'm so glad you called. How are you doing?"

"I'm okay. Tired, but okay. And a lot of people save Sunday for family. Or church. I don't know..." Her voice trailed off.

"Nah, I'm all alone. Not much of a church guy either, so you're good. And like I said, I'm glad you called. You're all I can think about. I've been so worried. I wish I could be there with you. I hate that you're having to go through this alone." I wrapped a towel around my waist and went to sit on my bed while we talked.

"I'm not alone. My assistant has been here. She's great. And William's assistant came by earlier. She's really nice too. He didn't always get along with her, but she's loyal and smart. She'll make a good candidate to replace him now."

Bailey sounded so detached it was unsettling. I was starting to recognize it was how she handled heavy emotion. She just shifted into autopilot and became very businesslike. Very robotic.

"Wait. What are you saying? Has your husband—?" I stopped mid-question, not quite able to bring myself to ask if he'd passed.

"No. Not yet. Not technically, at least. The doctors say there is no brain activity now. We...well, I will have to decide how long he will remain on life support. I know his wishes were to not live this way, so I need to respect that. I just need to prepare a statement, make sure some details are handled first."

I wasn't sure I was hearing her right. And I wasn't sure I

could wrap my head around it if I were. In one moment she was talking about taking her husband off life support, and in the next breath, she was worried about a press release and his successor at his job. What a fucked-up reality. Was she really that cold inside, or had life in politics warped her?

I flashed back to our dinner at the Kimpton. Bailey had made reference to hiding behind a mask, that when the light shone just right, you caught a glimpse of the real her. Was that actually a warning? Was the underbelly of the political world she lived in alongside her husband so dark and mutated that nothing, or rather no one, was who they appeared to be?

"Are you still there?" Bailey's question brought my attention back to our phone conversation.

"Yeah. I'm here. Sorry," I said. "I'm just...yeah. Sorry. I wish I had something better than that." The good manners ingrained in me as a boy and the natural empathy that was just part of my elemental makeup overrode the alarm bells sounding in my head, and I went with what my heart told me was right. "What can I do for you now, though? I feel so impotent stuck here. Is there really no way I can be there with you? A friend of the family in the media's eye?" I asked hopefully. There was just no denying it. I was head over heels for her. The thought of being able to see her again, in any capacity, energized me.

"Hmmm. That might work. And we can twist it into something if we think hard enough. Say you were working with William on some public outreach project or something since your face is so recognizable. I mean, I would really like to see you. It would be so good to be with you right now."

Interesting, the differences in the woman I cared about.

There was the one who let her guard down and said the last statement. Then there was the good politician's wife who said she was fine and that her assistant was there and handling everything. It was hard to reconcile the two, and if she and I continued to explore a relationship with each other, we were going to have to set some ground rules about hiding behind that mask of hers.

Suddenly, something smacked me in the face like a glass of ice water.

"Your husband is William Hardin? The city manager?" I croaked.

"Yes. Why do you ask? Haven't we talked about that before?"

"Shit." I rubbed the back of my neck, feeling the tension grip me like fingers.

"What's wrong?" Her voice grew tighter in response to mine.

"Skye Delaney is his assistant." The words came out like a robot, a statement rather than a question.

"Yes, she's a lovely woman. Do you know her?" she spoke slowly, trying to find the meaning in what I was saying.

"She's my best friend and roommate." There was no sense being obtuse. And that also explained where Skye had been for the past almost two days. So much for the killer hangover.

"Oh." There was a moment of silence while Bailey put some mental pieces together. "Have you told her about us? I mean, how we met and all?" I wasn't shocked that's what she homed in on as most worrisome. Image above all else, after all.

"No. I didn't even know your last name. I mean, she knows

what I've been doing to make ends meet. But no, I didn't tell her that I met someone I cared for—that our first encounter was through Book Boyfriend. I haven't really seen her a whole lot lately. To be honest, your husband kind of runs her ragged."

The moment the words left my lips, I wished I could recall them. I had gotten in such a habit of bad-mouthing Hardin, I didn't pay mind to whom I was speaking or the situation at hand. Just being a first-class—or classless—asshole, thank you very much.

"I shouldn't have said that. I'm sorry. Such an idiot." I silently banged my head against the wall of my bedroom a few times in self-flagellation.

"No, it's true. William has always been a workaholic. It's probably one of the things that led to his heart condition. I'd been bugging him to see a doctor recently. He'd put on weight, and the stress of campaign season is tough on everyone. If a mayor is elected who doesn't have faith in him, he'll be replaced. I'm sure you see it with Skye too."

"She thrives on it, though. It scares me a little, actually. I think she seeks out stressful situations sometimes just for the thrill of it. Like an adrenaline junky. At least she takes care of herself otherwise. I try to feed her healthy food, but the girl loves bacon like a red-blooded American farm boy." I laughed, thinking of the breakfast I'd made her to atone for my selfish behavior just a few days ago.

My smile held for a few more seconds while I listened to Bailey share a story of when she first met Skye. I was glad to hear they'd always had an easygoing relationship and that Hardin had a higher regard for her than he let on.

"Okay, I need to get back inside. I've been sitting outside on this little stoop I discovered. It's nice when I just need to regain my composure. I think we're going to do a press conference first thing in the morning. Skye is working with the PR team now." She paused and let out a big yawn before quickly excusing herself. "Gosh, excuse me. I'm exhausted. I'll probably sign the papers here in a little while. The doctors don't hold out a lot of hope once they turn the machines off." Her voice trailed off. Really, what more can you say after something like that?

"Are you sure you don't want me to come down there? I could probably be there in less than an hour." I couldn't imagine facing something like she was alone.

"And you really wouldn't mind?" Her voice was small again, the vulnerable Bailey showing.

"No. Not at all. I'd much rather be there than pacing a path in my carpet here." I started shuffling through my closet for something to wear while we talked. I still had a towel wrapped around my waist from the shower.

"Will you contact Skye to get you up to the floor? Security is very tight, but she can handle the details for you." All-business Bailey was back, and it took me a second to catch up with my own answer.

"Okay. I'm so glad you said yes."

"But Oliver, please understand. I'm his wife. This is not going to be all holding hands and canoodling in the corner."

"Did you really feel like you needed to tell me that, Bailey?" The fact that she even said it out loud pissed me off. I was trying to be understanding under the circumstances, but

I wasn't insensitive or an idiot. I was very well aware of how easily people could judge the moral soundness of the situation between us.

"No. I guess not. I'm just trying to stay in control of the things I can control, I guess." Her tone was much less sermonizing now.

"Well, take me off that list. It's not necessary, nor will it ever be." Barely tempered anger clawed at my throat.

She ended the call quickly. "I'll see you soon."

"Bye." Damn, I wished she hadn't said that. I was so pissed when I hung up my phone, I wanted to throw it on the ground and stomp on it instead of dial Skye and make a whole bunch of effort to appear to be something I wasn't. I fully understood the need to keep up appearances for the media, but being chastised like a child needled my empathetic mood.

Quickly finishing in the bathroom, I gathered a few things, threw them in my backpack, and called for a ride. Several cars were in the area, so the wait was short. Skye called as I was getting in the back seat of Bill's Blue Lexus.

"Hey."

"Hi. I guess I'm going to be meeting you in the lobby of Cedars?"

"Yeah," I said somberly.

"Why do you sound like I'm saying the lobby of the city's gas chamber?"

"I don't know. Wait! Our city has a gas chamber? Seriously?" Even Bill glanced in his rearview mirror when I asked that.

"No, we don't. I think San Quentin is the only one. And I'm

not sure they've used it in a really long time. Mid two thousands, maybe? But you're totally distracting me with nonsense, and you know it. What's going on outside of this bizarre six degrees of William Hardin game we have going on?"

"I know, right? How did I not figure this out sooner? I never even asked her what office her husband was in. I didn't really care, to be honest."

"So are you into her?" Skye asked, truly interested in the affairs of my heart. Just as I would be hers.

"I think I am." I could feel the grin spreading across my face. "Yeah, I totally am. She's so different than other women I've dated."

"Dated, Oll? Really? Can you even use that word with a straight face?"

"What?"

"When's the last time you saw the same woman more than once? Intentionally?"

Oh, she had to go and throw that curveball in there. While Skye had a point, it wasn't really my fault. When I was modeling, I traveled so much. It just wasn't a lifestyle suited for settling down.

At least that's what I told myself.

Apparently I had taken too long to answer by my roommate's estimation. "Mmmm-hmmm, that's what I thought," she said. "Don't go jumping the gun here, Oliver. I really don't want to see you get hurt. I'm not sure Mrs. H is really the gal you think she is."

"How could you even know what I think she is and is not? Why would you even say something like that?" The anger that had been sparked by Bailey's earlier comment was quickly reignited by Skye.

"I don't know. I hear that dreamy white picket fence tone in your voice, and it's making the hair on my arms stand up. I just want you to keep your wits about you. Especially right now. She's going to be vulnerable as shit now, and I don't want you to get all caught up in it."

"Not everyone is commitment-phobic like you are, Skye." Only best friends could get away with speaking to each other the way we did.

"That's not a word. And how can you even be saying the C-word already? If you got involved with Bailey through your current side hustle—which shall not be mentioned... I mean, really, do you hear yourself? She paid you to have sex with her, Oliver. Not fall in love with her," she volleyed back.

"How we met doesn't particularly concern you. And, while I'm pointing out the obvious: taking advice from you— the one who has oh so much experience in the romance category—makes perfect sense. I'm about three blocks away, so I'll see you in a few minutes." I disconnected the call before she could argue further or make any more assumptions about my feelings for Bailey. God, these women were infuriating me!

There were definitely things about Bailey Hardin that gave me pause. Her being vulnerable or needing someone to lean on weren't on that list. The way she shifted her emotions on and off was numero uno. Right underneath came the control issues. I wasn't a big fan of being told what to do or how to do it. Those two personality traits summoned mental images of my father, and consequently, my spine stiffened.

Lastly, if getting involved with a woman who was used to living different versions of her life depending on the audience she was living in front of meant I had to do the same thing, I wasn't sure I would be able to set all the things that mattered to me aside and do that.

Being authentic and dependable in a relationship was paramount to me. Trust, integrity, and honesty would have to be foundation words our relationship was built upon. Changing who you were in order to fit into certain people's ideals just seemed, well, fake. And if I wanted phony bullshit, I could just keep sleeping around with the kind of girls I had been seeing my whole life up to this point. I was ready for something different, and I was really hoping Bailey was that something.

Skye met me in the lobby as promised, and we shared a quiet ride to the sixth floor. The hallway was still when we stepped off into the dimly lit space. At the far end, the glow from an open door spilled out into the corridor, a few people milling about in the shadows. The odd scent combination of stale coffee and pine floor cleaner filled the air and turned my stomach within a few minutes of standing in the hallway. Hospitals have a creepy way of invading all your senses at once, confusing your system and setting your nerves on edge.

"He's in that room," Skye said quietly. "Bailey's in there now. The doctors are waiting for her to leave, and then they will turn off the machines. She said she wanted to say goodbye first and then walk away. She didn't want to be in there and make a 'tragic scene,' as she called it." She made air quotes around the last few words and rolled her eyes, apparently not agreeing with the choice.

"Who are we to judge at a time like this?" I said, matching my volume to hers to not attract attention.

"Oh, spare me the righteousness, Oliver. If I had come home and told you this same story and you hadn't had your dick in her, you would've been on my side one hundred percent." The acid in her voice was incongruent with the moment.

"You're probably right. And look how unfair that would've been of me. Have you even stopped for a second and put yourself in her shoes?" I answered quietly.

She just stared at me before dropping her folded arms from across her chest and walking on farther down the hall toward Hardin's room. I figured I'd be better waiting where I was for the moment.

About twenty minutes passed before Bailey came out of the room and toward me in the hallway. I waited for some sort of cue from her, and she made it very easy by reaching for me with outstretched arms, so I gladly wrapped her in my embrace and held her while she sobbed against my chest. All eyes were on us, some openly staring, others sneaking glances when they thought I wasn't looking. Some thought they were being clever and were hiding their privacy invasion, but I had their number too. Nothing to see here, people. Just one friend comforting another.

When the doctor came out of the room about five minutes later, industriously followed by two nurses, each splitting off in a different direction, he quietly came to where I stood with Bailey. She straightened up, completely severing any physical contact we might have still had, and tidied her track suit jacket.

I hadn't noticed before, but she was still wearing the same clothes she had had on at my place two nights before. She managed to still look polished and composed without having a shower or likely a wink of sleep since. With Bailey Hardin, it was her bearing rather than what she was wearing that gave her the air of importance.

"We turned everything off. It was only a minute or so before he passed. I just wanted to tell you." He reached for Bailey's hands and held them in his own, seeming sincerely sorry for the loss of her husband's life. "You have my, and the entire staff's, deepest condolences, Mrs. Hardin. Please allow our grief counselor to sit with you and help in any way she can." He turned to introduce the freckle-faced woman who joined the small grouping, "This is Shelby. She can help make arrangements, prepare a service, contact out-of-town relatives, anything you need. Please utilize her services." He dipped his head in my general direction and then walked away.

I touched Bailey's arm to get her attention before Shelby launched into her spiel, which, judging by the size of the notebook in her arm, was going to be a long one. "Can I get you some coffee or tea? Water? Have you eaten?"

"You know what, I'd love some tea. Maybe chai if the café is still open downstairs in the lobby? I think Skye knows where it is, if you ask her." She smiled halfheartedly.

"I'll see what I can do." I squeezed her hand and turned in a circle to look for my best friend. She was down the hall a bit, just outside of Hardin's door. Honestly, why weren't they closing that thing and giving the man a little privacy in his passing?

"I'm going to go get Bailey some tea. Do you want anything?" I leaned in closer and mumbled, "Shouldn't you close that door out of respect for the guy? Who knows who could just walk by here?"

"Good call. We're supposed to have the floor to ourselves, but you never know. This isn't a floor they normally put admissions on. That reminds me..." She reached into her messenger bag and pulled out a badge for me to pin on. "That will allow you to come and go from this area. If anyone asks for credentials, just say you're a family friend."

"Family friend." We recited the words together, and I rolled my eyes.

"In addition, I'd love an Americano with tons of milk if they're still open in the lobby. I didn't check their hours, but I feel like shit with the hangover and little sleep."

"So how long have you been here?" My guess was the whole story about being at Laura's was bullshit.

"Shit...what day is it now?" She frantically scrolled through her phone as though she might have missed an important appointment.

"Sunday evening," I mumbled.

"Damn...and I went out with Laura and the girls Friday, so since Saturday morning?" She gave a quick whiff past her armpit. "Still good. Nowhere to shower either. I think we'll be moving base camp soon anyway."

"Why didn't you just tell me the truth? You didn't have to lie and say you were at Laura's the whole time when I texted you. I was genuinely worried." The mixture of hurt and anger twisted in my gut. Couldn't anybody in this political world just be who they said they were? And hello? This was the city manager, not the fucking POTUS.

"Don't look so butt hurt, Oll. You know how this game is played. Some things are on a need-to-know basis. And until the queen bee over there gave the word, all lips were sealed." She motioned toward Bailey with her chin.

"And by the queen bee, you mean because she's the next of kin?"

"Please." She scoffed like I was the village idiot.

"What? You have to catch me up. You forget, I don't actually know how this game is played. I'm not usually one for games at all."

"That woman has been calling the shots in his career since they were in college. She's the one who got him the city manager job. She and the mayor go waaaaayyy back. And as you know, the mayor appoints the city manager. From here, she was gunning for state senate and then probably governor. If I play my cards right, she will whisper in her friend's ear about me stepping in to finish the term, and if Swanson is reelected in November, I may just be able to hold the job through his next term too." It was a toss-up which was more disturbing— the hunger in her voice or the gleam in her eye.

"Jesus Christ, Skye." I honestly felt sick to my stomach listening to her plot.

"What?" She recoiled a half step, affronted that I wasn't fully on board.

"Well, I can't be sure, but I don't think the body is even cold yet. Were you up last night planning this shit out by the light of his vital signs monitor?" My words came out in a series of hisses.

"That's funny, Oliver." Her deadly serious tone was in complete opposition with her words.

"I'm not joking." My tone matched hers.

"No, literally *funny* because your hot little number over there is the one who laid it all out to me—by the light of *her* dying husband's vital signs monitor. I'd really love that coffee, though, if you're still fetching one for her."

I stood there gaping at her back as her hair swung into position from the abrupt turn she made as she walked away.

Holy shit.

What was I getting myself into? These two women were cobras in a basket, and the only man who had the charmer's pungi lay lifeless on the opposite side of the door I was kind enough to insist be closed in preservation of his dignity.

CHAPTER TEN

Janine and I met in the complex gym bright and early Monday morning. I had barely slept after I got home from the hospital, but I needed to expend some of the nervous energy pinging around inside me.

We had the place to ourselves, so it was a great time to talk about Book Boyfriend Inc. We came up with a plan while we worked out, dividing tasks so we could finish what needed to be taken care of to get up and running quicker. The sooner BBI was a legitimate business, the better. I had to take care of certain things as the owner, and since I didn't have a car, she offered to loan me hers.

"I'd feel a lot better if you just drove me. I'd hate if something were to happen to your car. Your husband would lose his shit if he found out some guy was cruising around in your seven series." I watched her halfhearted attempt at a yoga pose I'd seen Skye do a thousand times while I worked my traps on one of the machines.

She panted while straightening to stand. "My husband doesn't need to know, for starters, and if I'm carting your tight butt around all day, I won't be here getting things done on my own list, will I?"

I twisted at the waist, trying to get a better view of my own backside, just to tease her.

"Trust me on this one, Oliver. It's tight." She shook her head and rolled up her yoga mat. "So, we'll meet back at your place by two? That should give you enough time to get done at city hall and me more than enough time to deal with the printer and the fictitious-name filing requirements. I'm going to look into web designers too if I get done early. We really need an internet presence."

"Yeah, I don't know about that. Sounds expensive." Draining the last of my water, I admitted the inevitable. "I may need to work in a couple dates this week. I've been paying more attention to my personal life, and the requests are backing up."

Janine was the only person outside those involved who knew the entire story regarding Bailey and Skye. I had to have someone to confide in, and now that Skye was changing her temperament as fast as the tide changed down at the pier, I wasn't feeling like she was an unbiased party anymore.

"How is Bailey going to feel about you"—she paused, probably searching for a tactful term—"*dating* other women?"

"She's known about Book Boyfriend this whole time. She's never once said don't do it anymore. I need to pay my bills, Janine. And have you heard me take a call from Harrison lately?"

"What if the client wants to sleep with you? Are you prepared to turn them down?"

We walked slowly across the complex, following the winding sidewalk still wet from the overnight sprinklers.

"I hadn't really thought of that. I guess I'll have to address it from the initial arrangements."

"Don't you think that will eliminate some prospective clients? I think you need to start farming out, Oliver. You said you had a few friends you thought about hiring. If we are taking this operation bigger, you won't be able to go on all the dates yourself anyway. No time like the present, right?" She stopped walking and turned to face me directly. "But this brings up another thing I wanted to talk to you about. Do you know what an angel investor is?"

"No, not exactly." I quickly tried to deduce the meaning from the two separate words themselves. "Is it money left to a company in someone's will?" Maybe she was forgetting the little detail that I wasn't the best with money matters.

"Not quite. It's a person who invests in a business but is totally hands-off. They literally front money, and that's it. They want nothing else to do with the business other than a return on the money they put in." She waited to make sure I was still with her, ducking her head down for assurance I understood. I had had my fill of her insulting my intelligence overall.

Maybe it was lack of sleep, maybe just too much stress in general, but I cracked. "I'm not an idiot, Janine. Just because I have a pretty face doesn't mean there's a rock instead of a brain. It doesn't have to be a brain *or* good looks. I'd appreciate if you'd stop treating me that way."

She took a step backward and looked at me like I had completely offended her.

"What? Are you going to say you haven't been treating me that way?" I was still angry but lowered my voice. It was early in the morning, and my deep voice reverberated off the stucco exterior of the condos.

"No, not at all." She put her hand up to her chest and patted a few times. "I'm going to say thank God you finally stood up for yourself. I was wondering how long it was going to take you. Do you always let people walk all over you like I've been?"

What the... "So you've been testing me?"

"Yeah. I don't want to be in business with some wussy boy. I want to know that you're going to stand up for us if need be. I've been insulting you for weeks, and you just take it. Let that be a lesson to you." She pushed my shoulder with an open hand, knocking me off balance because I wasn't expecting the contact.

I looked at her sideways. "You're a strange lady. Maybe I was just raised with better manners than you're used to from all these surfer boys. My mother would've washed my mouth out with soap if she heard me speak to one of my elders with such disrespect."

"Well, in business you need to stand up for yourself. Manners are all fine and good, but don't let someone else walk all over you. Verbally or otherwise. And excuse me? Elders?"

She was grinning when I looked up from the sidewalk I'd been studying for the better part of her lecture. "I'm glad we've settled all that. But seriously, think about it. I have an angel investor lined up for BBI."

"Okay, let me think while I'm doing these errands today. I know what you're offering is amazing, but I also know my head isn't screwed on straight right now. I need time to think." When I met her stare again, she was more serious, but concern and understanding had replaced the teasing look.

"We'll come up with something," I assured her. And I truly believed that. Above all else, I knew this business idea was solid. After the way I felt doing that last shoot, I was pretty sure my heart wasn't in modeling anymore, either.

"I'm not certain where things stand with Bailey. That shit Skye told me really has me looking at both of them in a different light. I'm not sure I know them at all."

"Would you even be convincing right now with a client? I don't know." She shook her head in doubt and continued. "I know you're really stressed out. I just think you may want to think about turning clients away instead of wrecking the company's image because you're not giving them what they're looking for. They're already used to not being fulfilled at home. You know?" We walked the rest of the way to my front door while we talked and then stood in front of my unit for a few more minutes.

She was making very good points. Nothing I hadn't already thought of myself, but I quickly dismissed it because other, more immediate problems came pushing and shoving their way to the forefront. That's how I currently dealt with life. Like a battlefield corpsman, triaging injuries. The non-anesthetized amputees were dealt with swiftly while the minor contusions waited outside the tent. Janine and I agreed to check in later that afternoon after we finished our to-do lists.

◆ ◆ ◆ ◆

What I thought would be a few days of hiatus from seeing Bailey turned into two weeks. We sneaked a rendezvous in when we could, but the scandal surrounding her husband's death had turned all eyes to her. She became a media darling, the curious public watching to see how the poor aggrieved wife was handling the shame her husband left behind for her to deal with. Of course, the reality was far different from what played out on the news, but she would ride the wave until the next news event caught everyone's attention.

"How can you keep watching this shit?" Skye snatched the television remote from the coffee table and turned the set off before I even looked up from my laptop, barely registering she was in the room.

"Huh?"

"So intelligent, Oll. You need to leave the house. Your brain is rotting in here without fresh air."

"I'm working. I have to come up with a schedule for next week for Janine by..." I took a quick look at my phone for the time. "Shit, I was supposed to be done with this twenty minutes ago. I'm going to have to hire more guys." I shook my head as my sentence trailed off.

"How many do you have on staff now?" she asked around a mouthful of cereal. My days of cooking for her ended about two weeks ago. I was just too busy with my own stuff now to wait on her. She was burning the midnight oil at the office anyway, most nights coming home well after I was asleep.

"I don't need a lecture right now, Skye. Thank you, though." I was tired and frustrated, and while she wasn't the cause of either, I had very little patience left for her judgmental attitude when it came to BBI.

"I wasn't going to lecture you. I'm genuinely curious." She tilted the bowl up to her mouth to drink the milk left behind.

"Four, not including me, but I haven't been out with a client since I met Bailey. So, yeah, four." I continued typing, not really caring if she responded.

"And you got an actual business license for pimping them out?" she asked over the rim of her bowl.

"It's a dating service, Skye. It's legal. And yes, I did." I was so not in the mood for her jabs. She used to support me when no one else did. But now, whether it was the business concept she disliked or my relationship with Bailey she didn't approve of, something had definitely shifted in the air between us.

"Did you write up a business plan?" she called from the sink, where, wonder of all wonders, she was washing her own dish and spoon.

"Yes. Why all the questions? Are you looking for a side hustle? City Hall not all you were hoping?"

"Very funny. I'm just impressed." She left the dishes to dry in the teak dish rack on the counter.

I stopped what I was doing and raised my stare to her waiting one. "I'm sorry? Come again?"

"*Impressed*, Oliver. I know it's not a word you hear from me very often. But there, I said it. *Twice*. Nice going. You took an idea you truly believed in and ran with it. Good job, you." She nodded in approval, probably of herself, for doling out praise to the lesser man, but still, I wasn't going to ruin the moment.

"Thank you, Skye Blue. I know that all but killed you to say, but I still appreciate it." I watched her with narrowed eyes, as something told me there was more to the compliment.

She let her shoulders slump, physically hinting at

surrender. "I want the best for you. You have to know that. I love you."

"Mmmm-hmmm." Usually it took half a bottle of vodka to get her talking that way. The L-word didn't come across those lips without a price. I couldn't help but feel suspicious. Definitely wasn't falling for it.

"Don't be like that. We've been through so much together. Haven't we?" Her voice shifted to little-girl-Skye. Also, typically only brought out by alcohol.

"Yet, sometimes, I feel like I don't really know you at all." I was done playing. I wasn't sure what she was up to, but I didn't want any part of it.

"What's that supposed to mean?" She snapped out a hip, hands planted on either side. So much for surrender.

"Nothing," I said calmly and went back to typing on my keyboard. If she'd come around the other side of the sofa, she would have seen I wasn't even in an open document anymore. I just wanted to make my point and then shut the discussion down by appearing occupied.

A while back, when I first met Bailey, she had said something about Skye having to toughen up if she wanted to have a career in politics. That it wasn't a place for the faint of heart—something along those lines. I no longer worried about my best friend. She could go toe-to-toe with the best of them, and I'd fear for her opponent more. She didn't need a man to take care of her like I once teased. In fact, I don't think I'd stand by and let one of my gender stumble into that minefield without proper warning and safety gear first. Manville didn't need another soldier down, and after what I'd seen of her behavior lately, that would be the exact outcome.

My phone rang, and I recognized the burner phone number Bailey used. I purposely didn't change the contact name in case my phone was taken by someone thinking they could get information about her through me. Everything had to be reconsidered now. Every move and every thought had to be carefully evaluated for risk and reward before being executed. I grabbed my phone and laptop and went into my room, closing the door behind me. Skye would know who it was by that action alone, but she could suck a bag of dicks for all I cared at that moment.

"Hey, beautiful." I hadn't realized how much I'd been hoping she'd call until I saw it was her.

"I'm not so sure you'd say that if you saw me right now. Seriously, worst day ever." She sighed into the receiver.

"Why? What's going on? And how can I make it better?"

"I really don't know how you are so sweet and so single. It just doesn't add up. Do you turn into a big smelly ogre in the moonlight?" she asked playfully.

"Well, you've seen me in the moonlight. What did you think?"

"Hmmm. No, definitely not smelly." She laughed a little bit but trailed off too soon.

"Okay, seriously, tell me what's going on." I flopped back on my bed, squishing the pillow under my head to prop me up.

"Just the press. They won't let up. I just wanted to have my hair done. That shouldn't be too much to ask. My roots are a disaster, and the salon can't deal with all that commotion going on out front of their store, you know? It scares away other customers. The owner called the police, but the bastards just circled the block a few times and came right back when they saw the cops move on to more important calls."

"That does suck. I'm sorry that's what your day was like." I wished I had something better to offer than sympathetic words, but really, what could I say?

"And I know, total first-world problems, right?" She chuckled, using a teenage girl dialect.

"I didn't say that. Didn't even think it."

"Well, you're sweet, that's why. But I feel like a brat even saying it. There are people in the world with way more serious problems than gray hair showing."

"Wait. You have gray hair? Oh...that changes things, Bailey. I'm not sure—" I teased.

"Shut up!" Then she laughed a little longer, and I smiled, hoping the teasing at least lightened her mood a little.

"It won't last forever. The media has a very short attention span. Something juicier will come up in the news, and they will be like a cat with a laser pointer and be off to chase the bright light." Trying to sound optimistic and pointing out the crappy habits of the media seemed like an odd combo, but it was definitely their pattern.

"So true. So true." She let out a big sigh. "Tell me about your day. What did you do with your time?" Bailey asked, clearly looking for a change of subject.

"I spent a lot of time rearranging the schedule for next week. Now that we have four guys to juggle, it's getting a little complicated. I try to match the clients up with who I think will best fit their requests, so it just takes a little time. Then, just when I think I have it all worked out, I either realize I forgot one request, or someone calls with an appointment they forgot to tell me about, or Janine tells me she already promised one of the guys somewhere else. It's maddening. But again, like you said, first-world problems." I did my best to emulate her teenage girl tone on the last sentence.

"Oliver?"

"Yes, baby?"

"I'm so proud of you."

And for the first time, maybe ever, it felt like someone said those words and meant them. It was hard to talk around the enormous lump that swelled in my throat.

"Did you hear what I said?" Her voice was so steady, I was afraid to answer, knowing mine would be anything but.

"Yeah. It's just hard." I gulped down the emotion squeezing my throat like a python.

"I know, but you're doing it. And it sounds like you've got a great handle on it."

Even after clearing my throat, I still answered roughly. "No, I mean, it's hard to hear that."

Of all the times in my life to be missing my family, I guess this was one of the worst. I was trying to deny it to myself, but Bailey's praise brought it all right to the surface. I knew they were never thrilled that my so-called fame came from looking good. That it wasn't a skill, or talent, it was a genetic gift that I chose to cash in on. Even then, I screwed up and blew through the money I made and didn't plan well for the future. I don't think I ever heard words of praise from either of my parents' mouths, so when she said them, I was really caught off guard.

"Why? What do you mean? It's true. I feel so proud of you."

"No one has ever said that to me. Or at least said it and really meant it. That just seemed... I don't know. It just felt like you meant it." The exchange between Skye and me moments ago felt completely disingenuous compared to this.

"Of course I did. I wouldn't have said it if I didn't. But it makes my heart sad that your parents didn't nurture you the way parents are supposed to."

"Well, they did the best they could. That's what I tell myself, at least. They were young when they had me. Had no actual plans of becoming parents so soon after getting together. My dad resented me my whole life for ruining his."

"Please, God, please tell me he didn't actually say those words to you."

"Okay, I won't tell you that." I just let silence fill the phone line. It always sounded so much worse when I told the story to someone else. I guess I'd built up some sort of protective shell against the awfulness of it.

"You poor boy. I wish I was there holding you in my arms."

"I wish you were too but for completely other reasons." I couldn't help but rub my cock through my pants. We were having to go way too long in between times we could see each other.

"Oh, I like the sound of that even more." Finally, her voice picked up excitement. Our phone conversation had gotten way too heavy.

"Right? Can we meet somewhere? Can I just come over? Are you alone?" Some nights, her personal assistant came over to help with errands or chores around the house or just to keep her company.

"Actually, I am. How soon do you think you could be here?"

I was already pulling up the Uber app while she was talking. There were usually drivers near my condo complex because we were fairly close to a shopping center.

"I'd say twenty minutes if the traffic gods are on our side."

"Please be discreet. Come around the back. I'll leave the garden gate open and the lights out. I'll even turn the pool lights out, so be careful."

"Oh, guess what? Perfect timing. The Emmys are tonight down by the Grammy Museum... Damn, what is the name of that theater now? Whoever paid to get their name on it—doesn't matter. What matters is all the paparazzi are going to be planted downtown, not at your gate."

"That's excellent news. Let's err on the side of caution regardless. I don't want to get cocky and be back in the headlines."

"Agreed. I'll see you soon. Wear something sexy!" Reenergized by the idea of seeing my girl, I zipped around my room, freshened up, and changed my clothes, leaving a wake of haphazardly strewn things all over the floor and bed. I knew I'd regret it when I came home to the mess later, but I couldn't bring myself to spend the extra time cleaning up.

I stuffed some things into my backpack with every intention of spending the night fucking Bailey into the mattress. We'd been holding off, waiting for the media vultures to go circle something else, and this might be our only chance for a while. I wasn't going to waste it. I made sure I had plenty of condoms in my bag, grabbed my wallet and phone charger, and went out into the living room. All the lights were out except the one we kept on in the kitchen overnight as a night light, so I assumed Skye had gone to bed. I checked my phone again to see how close my ride was and realized she was already out front. I quickly locked the front door and all but skipped to the waiting Prius in the parking lot.

The ride to Bailey's went quickly. I texted with her the entire way. Teasing and taunting her about what I had planned from the moment I walked in the door, I had a raging hard-on when I got out of the hybrid vehicle behind her large suburban home. A neighbor's dog barked in the distance when I closed the gate, but nothing out of the ordinary to arouse any suspicion.

When I got to the back door that led into the kitchen, I peeked into the window beside it and saw her waiting, pacing and glancing at her phone to see if I'd texted since we exchanged our last messages. I quietly turned the handle of the door, and she looked up, smiling the minute she saw me. After closing the door and sliding the three different locks into place, I pulled the blinds closed. When I turned to face her, she stood motionless, waiting and staring, wordlessly challenging me to make the next move.

Two strides and I covered her mouth with my own, bending her back, my hand woven through her loose hair, twisting my tongue with hers. I wrapped my arm around her waist, which seemed even smaller since I first met her, the stress of the past months showing in the neglect she punished her body with.

I felt like an animal, I was so hungry for her. So many days without touching her. So many hours spent in the same room pretending to be friends and nothing more. All the bottled-up attraction raged through my system and pounded through my veins, needing to be released in an aggressive show of ownership, of lust and need.

A scan of the surrounding room found a very large kitchen with a white marble island in the center. At the far end was an inlaid sink, and above that a pot rack with spotlights shining down on the gleaming surface. Beyond the kitchen was a formal dining room, floor-to-ceiling windows lining the far wall. Each window was adorned with heavy drapery, tied back at center points. We were definitely going to need privacy for what was about to go down, so I set her back from me by about a foot and grinned.

"Wait here. Don't move."

"Where are you going?" she asked, beginning to follow anyway.

"To close those drapes." I pointed toward the dining room. "If your neighbors are as nosy as mine, they may be inclined to call the police in a little bit, and we don't want to interrupt our fun, do we?" I didn't turn back to see her reaction, but when my words registered, I could hear her suck in air and halt her footsteps. As I was hoping, the drapes were tied back with silky braided cord, with large, decorative tassels on each end. Four windows, two panels each. I came back into the kitchen with eight cords in my hand.

I paused at the entrance back into the kitchen where Bailey had a small, built-in desk. The top surface matched the other countertops and blended seamlessly with the rest of the kitchen. Her sleek laptop sat in the center with the lid closed, personalized stationery lined up perfectly in the left corner of the desk. Christ, even her letterhead came to heel. I shook my head slightly, thinking how this woman even worked in the kitchen—a place where most families gathered and chatted about their days, nourished their hearts and souls with one another's presence. Her life needed a reboot, and I hoped like hell I'd be a part of the new landscape.

Toward the back of the desktop, an ornate canister glinted in the dim light that remained in the room. Little flowers made from wire scrolls adorned the cup that held pencils, pens, and a few markers. It was the one personal touch on the entire desk. Not a picture frame or Post-it note in sight. On impulse, I snatched one of the markers from the cup and stashed it in my back pocket, flipped all the lights off except the spotlights in the pot rack over the island, and strode toward Bailey, an idea germinating as I did.

"Oh, you could've just left those on the hooks on the sides of the windows. Here, I'll go put them back." She held out her hand for the lengths of rope, and a sinister grin spread across my lips. I shook my head before laying them out on the counter, making a big show of lining them up neatly, the burgundy color standing out in contrast against the white marble.

"Now. Where were we?" I turned to her and almost laughed at the alarmed look on her face. I didn't give her much more time to get worked up but pulled her against my body in one swift tug, pressing my erection into her and meshing our mouths in a deep kiss. By the time I let her up for air, her eyes were glassy and her pupils were almost as big as the iris itself.

"Mmmmm. That's what I thought. I'm going to set you up here." I patted the island, and she just looked at me, not agreeing, not disagreeing.

I grabbed her around the waist and easily popped her up onto the marble countertop. When I pushed my way to stand between her legs, we were nearly eye to eye. She had a small advantage above me.

"I have a bedroom, you know," she announced.

"Boring."

"I don't think any room you're in would be considered boring, Oliver." She wrapped her arms around my neck, locking her fingers together behind my head.

"Mmmm, sweet words from the lady. Are you trying to get me to do things your way?"

"No. I was just making mention of the fact that most people utilize a bed to, well, you know." She looked down, not comfortable talking about sex so blatantly.

"Fuck?" I, on the other hand, had no issue at all.

"Yes." She met my stare directly when she said it.

"Well, I'm not like most people. And I never want to be." I took her leg and bent it up at the knee, placing her flat foot up on the countertop so her heel was up against her ass cheek.

"What are you doing?" she objected.

"I'm going to have a little feast." I took one of the lengths of cord that held back the drapery only moments ago and then reached for her wrist. She watched me, confused but then enraptured, as I kissed and licked the sensitive skin on the inside of her wrist, swirling circles with my tongue before nibbling the thin skin with my teeth.

"Mmmmm, who knew that would feel good?" Her voice was just a whisper.

"See? You should trust me." I kept my eyes on hers while I took one last lick.

"I do," she said finally.

"Good. I'm going to tie your wrist to your ankle." I waited for my words to register.

"Wait. What? *What?*" She tried to pull her wrist from my grasp, so I let go.

"Easy. Sshhh." I kissed her lips, and she pulled back a little until I squinted my eyes in some version of disapproval. "If you thought what I did to your wrist felt good? Baby, you're about to have your mind blown. I'm not going to hurt you. I just want to play a little. You said you trust me." I held out my hand for her to give me her wrist back. I would wait there until she did it willingly. The night didn't have to go that way, but I was really hoping it would.

Finally, she let her desire win and trusted me to treat her well. She placed her wrist in my palm, staring in my eyes the entire time.

"You won't regret it. And next time, we won't have to go through this. You'll be asking me to do it."

"Oh, next time?" She chuckled. "We're already talking about next time? Mr. Confident." She rolled her eyes when I squinted again.

I secured her wrist with a quick loop of the silky rope and then the same around her ankle and attached the two to one another. She tested the binding, tightening the knots for me while doing so. I moved to the other side, and instead of kissing her wrist, I worked on the skin on the inside of her knee, causing a little yelp to escape from her when the torment got to be too much.

"God, how do you know these things? Wait. No! Don't tell me. Damn it, that feels so good." She let her head fall back while I secured her ankle to her wrist and stood back to survey the feast that awaited me.

Christ, if I could take a picture I would. But if she freaked out before, bringing out a camera phone would make her lose her shit. Another time, maybe. I gripped my cock again through my jeans, deciding I'd be much more comfortable with them off. I waited for Bailey to look at me and then made a show of taking them off. No underwear to bother with, so once the jeans were gone, it was all birthday suit for me. She still had on a little lace scrap of panty that was just making my fingers itch, and I couldn't decide the best way to eliminate it.

"How attached are you to these?" I ran my finger along the side of the crotch, letting the tip graze her swollen clit inside. She jolted from the minimal contact, glaring at me afterward.

"That's not a very nice look, young lady. Do you want to spend the rest of the night tied up like that while I jack off in front of you? Frustration can be a very painful state, you know."

"You wouldn't dare." She pretended to seethe.

I just toggled my head back and forth and then said, "I don't know... I wouldn't test it."

Swiping the knuckles of my fist down the center of her panties, I asked her again, "I'm thinking these need to go. Cut, rip, or stretch until they are useless. No matter how I see it, they're not going to survive the night."

"Please don't use sharp objects near my lady parts. Please *and* thank you." Her voice was saccharine sweet now.

"Your lady parts?" I laughed heartily. "Is that an actual hard limit for you? Like you will lose your shit? Or is it just mildly uncomfortable and you may actually be turned on by it? Or are you just being a control freak...as in, don't do it because I said so?" I tilted my head to the side and kissed her until we were both dizzy again. When we parted, I whispered, "Tell the truth."

"What are you doing to me?" she gasped.

"Do you like it?"

She gave a quick nod. If I hadn't been staring at her from an inch away, I might have missed it. The little grin on her swollen lips that followed assured me I wasn't just imagining what I wanted to be seeing.

"The first one," she blurted out. "But if I change my mind, will you stop?"

"Of course I will. We're here to enjoy ourselves, not freak out. What fun would that be?"

"Okay." She let out a big sigh. "Okay."

A big wooden knife block stood proudly beside the industrial-sized stove on the opposite side of the island. I strolled over to it and inspected several of the smaller knives that certainly would do the job just fine. Bailey twisted her body as best she could to watch what I was doing, so instead of practicality, I went for dramatic effect and pulled out the large chef's knife, the metal making a satisfying sound as it was pulled from its space in the block. I met her wide-eyed stare as I slid the knife back into the block and grabbed the kitchen shears instead. Watching her sag in relief, I knew that had been the better choice for this playdate. Maybe someday we'd have some fun with some of the other knives, but not tonight.

"These should do, yeah?" I looked from the scissors to her, waiting for her response. Her look was so trusting, I almost burst with pride. I would never actually hurt her, but something about the power play was totally turning me on, and the fact that she was letting me do it was taking it to an entirely different level.

My cock twitched, begging to be buried inside of the woman mere inches away. Restraint was going to be rewarded, though. I planted my hands on the outside of her hips and kissed a path down her neck. Goose bumps rose up on her skin in reaction when I paid particular attention to the area behind her ear.

"You like that."

"Mmmmm," was all I got in response.

I bit down gently, and her sound got deeper, letting me know that was a good idea. I moved with more kisses across her collarbone, gently nudging her to lean back so I could access her chest. Since her hands were tied to her ankles, she could only lean back so far before she had to lie down completely. Either that or have the best ab workout of her life. An idea took root in my imagination, and I decided to go for it.

"Lie back, baby."

She was already pretty blissed out, so she did what I asked without arguing. I kissed her again to keep her in the right place mentally, because I was about to really test her trust. Or really turn her on. It was only going to go one way or the other; there wasn't going to be a gray area in between.

While kissing her with all I had, I pulled the marker from my back pocket. A quick check confirmed what I was hoping— it was the washable type. The moment I pulled the cap off, she would know what I had in my hand. The smell these writing tools emitted was as identifiable as the solid black slashes the tip left in its path. But I needed to start as close to her collarbone as possible for what I had in mind. I pressed the tip against her pale skin and watched the flesh pucker around it.

I could've predicted the exact moment she would protest. Her eyes shot open, and she tried to sit up. I was ready, and I moved the marker away so she wouldn't inadvertently draw on herself.

"What are you doing?"

"Ssshhhh. I'm not going to hurt you. I'm drawing on your skin. You're like a commissioned work of art. An Oliver Connely original." I grinned lazily, imparting my calm vibe over her. "But if you jump up like that again, you're going to ruin my masterpiece." I waited for her to process what I'd said. "Lie back down. Let me do this."

When she finally decided to comply, I kissed her lips in gratitude. I made my way down her neck again, but this time I couldn't resist her breasts, standing proudly in the black bra she still wore. I quickly grabbed the scissors again and slid the blade under the delicate fabric between her breasts and made a quick snip, slicing the garment off with one motion.

"Well, that was easy. This thing is really sharper than I thought." I shrugged carelessly when her eyes widened again. Before she could launch into any sort of chastisement, I covered her mouth with a searing kiss, sweeping my tongue into her mouth deeply, probing and thrusting until she wilted back down flat to the marble counter.

"Now you need to stay very still. Can you do that, Bailey?" I whispered the words against her lips after kissing her.

She paused a second or two and then gave a shaky nod.

"And remember, if you don't want to play anymore, just say so and I'll stop. Okay?"

"Yes. Okay." This time she answered with words, and the tremble in her voice shot through my bloodstream like an electric current.

"Let me just check something, though." I unceremoniously shoved my hand into her panties and swiped my index finger through her folds. The moisture was so abundant, she wouldn't be able to convince me she wasn't completely turned on with any amount of protesting.

"Just making sure." I winked at her and sucked on my finger while she watched. "I can't wait to have my mouth on your pussy, Bay. So fucking good."

"Oliver. Please." Her voice was so sexy when she said my name that way.

"Soon, baby." I held the black marker above her sternum again so she knew I was going back to work. I was really going to see this through. She took a deep breath in, preparing for whatever I had in mind, and exhaled slowly.

Pressing the tip back into the starting point, I made a circle, pressing as evenly as possible over the hills and valleys of her ribs. When I met back at the top where I started, I stood back a little to admire my handiwork and was impressed. A quick check-in with Bailey, and while her face was a little tight, she appeared to be just fine and enjoying it.

I continued down the center of her body, drawing on her skin with the marker, alternating that with teasing her body with my mouth. She was flushed and very slick between her legs when I finished and set the marker down.

"What is it? What did you draw? I lost track of the lines?"

"You can look later. I have more important business to tend to."

I settled my mouth on her mound and went to town. She was so ramped up, she yelped when I finally gave her my full attention. I licked her clit, sucking her juices into my mouth and moaning when her taste hit my tongue.

"Damn, you taste so good. I will never get tired of eating you. Ever."

"Feels so good. Please. Please. Oliver. I need to finish. Please." Her begging turned to whining pleas.

"All right, baby, let's do it." I thrust two fingers into her hole and twisted them upward, reaching in deeper to hit the right angle to make her go over.

"God. Oh my God. Stop! What are you doing? Oh my God."

Jesus, this poor woman. How did she go this long in her life without being fucked properly? Of course I didn't stop. I pushed in farther and really stroked the smooth spot on the roof of her channel, sending her to heaven.

"Come, baby. Soak my hand." I urged her on while thrusting in and out of her pussy.

"Yes, Oliver. Yes. I'm coming." She keened into the darkness of her kitchen.

I could feel her tunnel tighten down on my fingers, spasms quaking her walls while she moaned my name. And when I looked up to her face, across her body, my cock surged harder than it ever had. For across the pale skin of her torso, now standing out in stark contrast, were the letters spelling my name.

"I need you, Bailey. Need to be inside you." I grabbed the tops of her thighs and dragged her toward the edge of the island until her ass was teetering over. I was tall enough to slide right into her if I didn't want to change the angle of my thrusts. I looked around the kitchen again quickly and spotted a table in the breakfast nook. Bingo, it was about a foot lower than the countertop height.

"Hold on, baby. We're moving." I scooped her up in my arms before she had time to process what I had said, causing a yelp from her. I kissed her nose when she looked up to me, "I just want to be at a better angle." I set her down on the table and pushed her knees back, rocking her whole body back on her spine.

"How's that? Comfortable?" I smiled, as her face was still flushed from her orgasm.

"It's going to be better in a second." She rubbed her cheek on one of my forearms, which were planted on either side of her head on the kitchen table.

"That's my girl." I pressed the head of my cock into her slick opening, watching her body accept mine greedily.

"God, woman. So good."

"I can't believe I'm having sex on my kitchen table." She closed her eyes, as if embarrassed.

"Of all the things that have happened tonight, that's the one that stands out, huh?" I chuckled, pressing fully into her.

"Oh, Oliver." Her bright-green eyes sprang open again. "Oh, yes."

"Yeah, baby. There we go." I pulled out and slid back in. Closed my eyes and just enjoyed the sensation. Her pussy gripped me tightly. I could die a happy man after having been inside this woman, having experienced what she gave of herself during lovemaking. The trust floored me. The generosity comforted me. The sensuality enraptured me.

I wouldn't last long. Between the nights I'd spent alone and the canvas she had allowed herself to become for me, I was already counting backward in my head to stave off my orgasm.

"Shit. God, Bailey. You're killing me. I need to come. I have to stop. Be still." I tried to hold her hips still, but she just kept squeezing me from the inside. "Brat. I'm serious. It's going to be over too soon. Then you'll have to wait too. Be still."

"It feels so good, Oliver. I don't want you to stop. Please. Please." She swiveled her hips when I let go, and I growled low in my throat. I bent over her and drove into her as hard as I could, moving her back on the table an inch or so. I wrapped my arms beneath her and held her in place for the punishing thrusts I delivered until I drained my seed deep within her, throwing my head back and moaning with her as we came together, our mixed sounds of pleasure bouncing off the walls of the empty kitchen.

Sweet perfection. I had found paradise. It wasn't an

isolated island in the tropics. It wasn't a mountain cabin retreat. It was a suburban kitchen, on a breakfast nook table, with the sexiest woman I'd ever had the honor of making love to. I nuzzled into the crook of her shoulder and neck and inhaled the scent of her skin and our mixed chemistry and tried to coax my heart and breathing to a calmer place.

Finally, I untied her ankles and wrists and rubbed the pink marks left behind. Helping her sit up, I grinned at the completely disheveled look she was rocking. I had never seen her with so much as a hair out of place. Even when we had had sex in the past, it was always neat and controlled, very orderly and proper.

"Now that was a nice and dirty fucking. It suits you." I kissed her swollen mouth and forced myself to pull back before I got started all over again.

"I don't think I can walk." She stood up and wobbled, so I quickly grabbed her arm for support.

"You look supremely proud of yourself," she said.

"I am. Shouldn't I be?"

"Actually, yes, you should. I'm dying to know what's going on here." She motioned to her torso where I had drawn on her flesh.

"Let's go take a shower, or even better—a bath. Then we can get some sleep. Then you can wake me up in the middle of the night with your mouth wrapped around my cock, and then we can fuck again, go back to sleep... Well, you get the idea."

She just stood there with her arms folded across her chest as if she disapproved of the plan.

"What?" I asked innocently.

"You have it all figured out, don't you?"

"Do you object to the proposed plan?"

She thought for a minute and then dropped her arms. "No. Not really." Then she took off running like a little shot, the last thing I had expected her to do. When I finally registered her action, I took off after her, both of us laughing like maniacs.

I caught up with Bailey in the upstairs hallway, where she was standing stock still in front of a full-length mirror staring at her reflection. Her fingers hovering over the letters I had written on her skin.

I didn't know what to say, so I waited for her cue. I watched her trace the letters with her finger, mouthing the word as she went. Finally, she met my eyes in the mirror.

"You wrote your name on me. On my flesh." Her voice was barely audible.

"Yes."

"Why?" Still, a whisper.

"I feel like you own me. My heart." My voice was quiet too, I didn't want to spook her. With my volume or my message.

"You do?" She finally turned to look at me directly instead of my image in the mirror beside her.

I nodded.

"Oh."

"Does that worry you?" I needed her to say more than "oh."

"I don't think so. I mean, it's soon, you know?" She looked back to our reflections. Maybe looking at the situation directly was too intense. "But I don't feel scared under here." She touched her own chest again, where her heart lay beneath.

"Good. That's good enough for me," I said. "For right now. That's good enough."

"This will fade?" She traced a few of the letters on her skin.

"Yes." I felt like the less I said at the moment, the better. She was clearly working through her feelings, and I needed to give her the space to do that.

"Will this?" She turned to me then and touched my chest, where my heart lay beneath.

"I don't think so. I mean, it's soon. You know?" I purposefully used the exact same words she had just used, so she understood their meaning.

We stood, naked in the hallway, in each other's arms for some time. Not speaking, not moving. Just being. Two people, trying to figure out where to go from the point they were at. Trying to believe life would point the way for us—we just had to give it time and trust the process.

Bailey and I spent the rest of the night alternating between sleeping and screwing, with a few various breaks for showering and eating thrown in to keep things interesting. We finally fell asleep for an extended period of time around three in the morning, not bothering with an alarm or caring about obligations for the following day.

Which apparently was a cardinal sin in the world of Bailey Hardin. She leaped out of bed in horror and, when she saw her reflection in the bathroom mirror, burst into tears.

"Hey, whoa...what's going on? What's wrong?" I sat up, still groggy with sleep.

"Look at me! Look at me. Look at this!" she repeated,

violently pointing to her torso. "It's still there! How am I going to leave the house like this, Oliver? What on earth were you thinking?"

"Uhhhh. Well. Were you not planning on wearing clothes? No one will even see it. And dare I ask what happened to all the 'my heart, your heart' talk we fed each other last night?" I tried to keep my voice quiet and level, like talking a spooked cat in off a ledge.

"Fed each other?" She turned from the mirror to square off with me. "Fed each other?"

"You know what I mean." Danger signs were popping up in my head like cartoon balloons above a character's head.

"No. I don't think I do. Why don't you explain it to me, Oliver?" She leaned back against the counter and crossed her arms over her chest, a body language move I was quickly getting used to of hers to mean "tread carefully, soldier—mine field ahead."

I held my hands out to her, palms up, an offering to her to place her hands in mine. A sign saying *trust me*. After a few seconds, she placed her small, trembling hands in mine.

"Why are you shaking? Are you cold?" I looked around the bathroom for a robe, since she was standing there naked.

"No, I'm angry. I shake when I'm mad." Her volume had dropped drastically.

"First of all, the marker isn't permanent. It said 'washable' on it. I actually checked before the idea became the runaway train it did." I dropped her hands in exchange for pulling her fully into my body. "I'm sorry you're mad."

Kissing her forehead, I continued. "I'm sorry something

I did made you mad. For the record, I don't regret a single minute of last night. I get hard looking at my name scrawled on your body like that." I pulled back to look at the faded lettering, not ready to release her just yet. "Yes, it's barbaric. Yes, it's possessive. But I like thinking you belong to me and I belong to you."

"I'm sorry I overreacted." She looked down, not able to meet my stare. "This is all very new for me. William and I were together for a very long time. I don't remember how this dating stuff goes." She laughed, trying to trivialize what was happening between us, I presumed. "I need to get in the shower and get ready to go to the office."

"I'm a little confused."

"About what?" She busied herself around the enormous bathroom, gathering various products and placing them in the shower.

"I didn't realize you had a job, I guess." I felt awkward admitting to not knowing everyday things about her.

"Of course I have a job." She looked at me like I'd just sprouted a second head.

"Well, what do you do?" I asked, genuinely interested.

"I work at city hall too. Didn't Skye tell you?"

"No. We haven't been on the best terms lately."

"Oh no. I hope that's not because of me." She left the bathroom and came back with a few towels in her arms.

"Why would you have anything to do with it?"

"I don't know. I just get the feeling she doesn't like me very much. I figured she might be filling your ear with office gossip." Bailey turned on the water in the shower and waited for it to get hot while we talked.

"I've never known Skye to get involved in office politics. I doubt she'd start now. She's way too driven." My voice trailed off, feeling bad about what I was saying, but knowing it didn't make it less true.

"That she is. I hope it doesn't hurt her in the long run." She got in the shower, and I watched her through the glass enclosure, entranced with the way the water caressed her breasts and hips as it ran over her skin.

"What do you mean?" I thought about what she had said and really wanted to hear her opinion about Skye's ambitious nature. She was still my best friend, and I knew how important her career was to her.

She stepped under the spray to rinse her hair, so I waited for her to resurface and finish answering my question.

"Well, sometimes being too focused on one goal in the future can make you blind to what's going on right under your nose. Does that make sense?" Her words were a bit muffled by the sounds of the shower, but I heard what she said.

"Yeah, I guess. Is there something I should be tipping her off about? I mean, she's my best friend."

"Nope. She has to find her own way in the game. That's how it all works, unfortunately. Sometimes we can nudge people or situations to go the way we want them to, but ultimately, we live in a democracy for a reason. Free will and all that good American dream drivel, you know?" She shut off the water and squeezed the excess water from her dark hair.

I handed her the towel she had set on the counter. The letters of my name were now just a faded gray shadow after her shower.

"Let me take care of you before I go." I pulled her by the hand into her room and pushed her down onto her bed.

"Oliver, no more. For one thing, I'm sore down there from all the 'care' you gave me overnight, and I'm going to be late as it is." She tried to sit up, but I didn't let her get very far. Such a stubborn woman.

I ignored her protests and took the lotion off the nightstand and then unwrapped the fluffy towel from her body, opening each half wide to either side of her. Kneeling down on the floor beside the bed, I put a generous amount of lotion in my palm and rubbed it together with my other hand, warming the lotion before holding my lubed hands above her.

"Close your eyes," I ordered softly.

"I'm going to be late," she protested again in response.

"Stop arguing with me and do what you're told, woman." I grinned down at her.

She huffed out a breath through her nose, sounding like an angry bull, and squeezed her eyes shut like a bratty toddler.

"Perfect," I said sarcastically and touched her nose with my creamy finger, and she giggled, relaxing all the attitude out of her face and body.

"I don't know why you insist on making everything so difficult," I said as I rubbed lotion on her body, being gentle and thorough with my attention to all the sensitive parts of her fantastic body. By the time her skin had absorbed all the balm from my hands, my cock was begging to find its way back inside her.

"I don't want to go to work now. See what you do to me when I give in? That's why I have to remain in control. Left to your devices, you would be much too dangerous for me, Oliver Connely." Her voice was husky and alluring, but I behaved and kept my attention to just the lotion.

I left soon after, knowing if I stayed, we'd be back in bed and she'd be calling in sick and then be pissed that I coerced her into it. Skye was already gone when I got back to the condo, and Janine had left three messages on my voice mail just that morning alone.

"Where have you been all morning?" she demanded the moment she picked up my call.

"I spent the night with Bailey. Mom?" I checked my display to be sure I hadn't misdialed. Usually she was the only one who got away with that type of questioning.

"We had interviews this morning with the new candidates. It should've been on your shared calendar. Wait, let me look..." There was a pause while she presumably looked through her own calendar, and I already knew what was coming next. "Oliver, if I go through the trouble of sharing a calendar event with you, you need to accept it so it gets added to your calendar as well. Then bullshit like this won't happen again. Okay?"

"Yes, Janine." I hoped I sounded as bored as I intended to sound. She was on my last nerve and totally killing the Bailey buzz from the past fifteen hours.

"If you're not going to take this seriously, I'm not going to waste my time or money on it either, Oliver. I'm serious. Just shoot straight with me. This has to be the priority over a piece of ass."

"You're treading on very thin ice right now. I'm sorry I missed the fucking interviews. I am. And I will accept the calendar events moving forward. But you have no right to speak about someone you don't even know in such a manner. Am I making *myself* clear?" Yep. That was me snapping like a twig under a Timberland.

"Perfectly," she fired back.

"And what do you mean, money?"

"What?" The abrupt subject change jarred her, but there was no sense beating a dead horse.

"You said money. Time *and* money," I explained.

"The angel investor." She paused. "Okay...fine, it's me. I never was good at keeping a secret, I guess. But I believe in this idea so much, Oliver. I just can't sit by and watch you screw it up. I'm sorry I was so short, but it's too important."

"It's everything to me too, Janine."

"It has to be, Oliver. It's the only way it's going to work."

"Stop stressing. Did you reschedule the interviews? I haven't received a new invitation, and I'm scrolling through email right now."

"No. I conducted them myself. We're calling back three of the seven."

"Really?" I was surprised. "Only three? Why?" I thought for sure at least five of my modeling friends were perfect fits for BBI.

"Let's talk about it in person. I'm coming over."

"I need a shower first. Give me twenty minutes." The last thing I needed was a lecture about smelling like sex and women's perfume from the night before.

"Okay, see you soon." Our call was done, but our business was just getting started.

CHAPTER ELEVEN

"Are you hearing a word I've said?" She tore the readers off the end of her nose and glared at me from across our small dining room table. It had become our conference room of sorts.

"Yes. Website. Web design. I heard it all. I really want you to just run with the project. I don't have any preference on the matter, Janine. I agree, we need one. I agree it will be the way almost every client accesses our services. I agree, it needs to be modern and classy but still young and fresh. I literally agree with everything you've said about it. Despite you saying about a million things. I just don't have anything to add. I trust you on this, one hundred percent."

I also couldn't get Bailey off the brain, but I was trying desperately to pull off this entrepreneur thing. I decided I didn't want to model anymore.

At all.

If Harrison called with a job, it would have to be something I literally couldn't turn down due to some contractual obligation in order for me to go on location again. I wanted to spend every night like I had the night before. I was falling in love with Bailey, and I wanted to spend my nights proving it to her.

"Jesus Christ. This is getting ridiculous. Do you want to

doodle her name on your notebook? Little hearts with your initials and hers? Then in different combinations?"

"What are you talking about?"

"I've been repeating the same question over and over, and you're staring off into space with a dopey look on your face. It's like goddamn junior high all over again," Janine barked at me.

"No, I wasn't," I defended.

"Totally were," she volleyed back. Then added, "Okay. Answer me this."

I just looked at her, bored and waiting for the telling question that would prove I was as lost in love as she insisted.

"How many times did you beat it in the shower before I got here?" Her matter-of-fact tone was almost more disturbing than the question itself.

Almost.

"What? Why on earth would I tell you that? Wait. No! Why would you even ask that?" I could not believe I was having this conversation.

"Because you're hopelessly in love. Or infatuated. One or the other. And that's the litmus test. I'm guessing an average day for a man your age is once? So if it was more than that?" She shrugged. "You're a lost cause. She already owns you."

I just stared at her, shaking my head, while she mouthed the words *owns you* again.

"You know I'm right. That's why you won't answer me. And you already said you spent all night with her. So, it's not like you had blue balls and it was a physiological necessity."

"I'm starting to hate you. Do you realize that?" I glared at her from across the table.

"No, you're not. You just hate that I'm consistently right. About everything." She put her reading glasses back on and picked up the paper she was reading.

"You need to stop." I felt like I was experiencing what it would be like to have an annoying little sister.

"Why? The truth is a hard pill to swallow?" She grinned at me from across the table.

"I'm serious," I repeated.

"He who has nothing to hide...hides nothing."

"Janine. Stop."

"I'm just telling it like it is, dude." She shrugged again.

"Three! It was three times! Fuck me! Are you happy now? Are you happy? Jesus motherfucking Christ! You are literally the most annoying fucking human I know."

She clapped her hands in front of her. "Awww, honey, you're in love. Isn't it the best thing in the world? All the feels right now?" She smiled so wide, and it was such an odd look, I didn't know if I wanted to burst out laughing or stand up and leave the fucking room.

"Did you just use the word 'feels' after badgering me into admitting I jerked off three times in less than fifteen minutes this morning? I don't even...yeah...I don't..." I stood up so abruptly, my chair toppled backward on two legs and smacked the wall behind it before dropping back down onto all four legs with a clatter. A deep dent was left in the drywall that Skye would zero in on the moment she came through the door after work.

"Wow. Three times? Fifteen minutes? No wonder these clients keep calling back asking for you. It's been a long time since my husband had that kind of stamina. Well, maybe he never did, the more I think about it."

"Janine." I held my hand up for her to stop. "Please. No. I can't take any more today. I'll beg if I have to." I flopped back down into the chair and just stared at her.

"I'm just happy for you. I love the idea of love more than anything, Oliver. That's why we all read these books in the first place." She pointed to one of the popular books we got character requests from, which was lying on her stack on the table. "Because we're all suckers for love. It keeps hope alive and passion burning strong. It's at the root of almost every other emotion. Whether it's twisted up and looks more like jealousy or betrayal and hiding behind hatred, it's always involved in one way or another."

We both sat in silence for a couple minutes.

"I'd never really thought of it that way. But you're exactly right."

"Again." She shrugged.

"Yes. Again." At this point I was just giving in to it. Arguing with her was pointless. I'd remember that for the future too. Hours of saved time coming my way.

"But can I ask you something? I'm curious to hear your opinion, since you clearly have tons of experience and I literally have none." Hopefully I wouldn't regret letting this mongoose out of the cage.

"Ask away." She closed her notebook and sat forward in her seat. Her enthusiasm was actually adorable.

"I'm concerned about Bailey and Skye. I feel like something bad is brewing between them." I threw my hands up and slid lower in the chair. "I don't even know what I'm saying. Like I don't know what that means when I say the words. It's more of a gut feeling."

"Well, let's break it down. What's making you feel that way? There must be something to it."

"I don't really know," I answered.

"That's bullshit. If you want my advice about something, Oliver, you have to shoot straight with me. In other words, I don't have some random bad vibe about, I don't know, say, you and my husband, because you are both men I know, and you are both men who are predominantly in my daily life. So, something must have happened, or was said by one of them, to give you bad juju about their relationship. Saying you don't know is a cop-out. An easy answer."

"I would've hated having you for a mother as a teenager. I'm just going to say that for the record."

"You know there's a saying... FBI agents have nothing on a mother with a hunch."

"Truer words have not been spoken." Was it possible to hate and love someone at the same time? I was pretty sure that's how I felt about this woman.

"Get back on track. Tell me what's really bothering you," she persisted.

"Okay, okay." I held my hands up to settle her impatience. "First of all, I found out this morning that Bailey has a job."

"Okay. That's not exactly state's evidence, Oll."

"I know, I know." I laughed. Maybe the whole thing would sound as absurd. "But it struck me as odd that I've known her this long and I didn't know she had a job. How hasn't that ever come up? And then she told me she works at city hall. So how in the hell hasn't Skye ever mentioned it either? They must see each other on occasion at least. And Skye was working for her husband up until recently."

"Hmmm. Okay. So that just made it a degree stranger. But still, it could be easily explained. Like Skye thought you knew already, and it wasn't something that necessarily would come up in your household conversation?"

"True. True." I agreed with her logic. To a point. Something still seemed odd.

"Aaaannnndd..." She drew the word out while she seemed to be coalescing her thought. "And you have said that you and Skye have been drifting apart since you've been seeing Bailey."

"Yeah. Unfortunately, it does feel that way."

"What else? I'm sensing you haven't addressed all your concerns yet."

"Are you fucking Yoda or something?" I changed my voice to sound like the green fuzzy swamp dweller. "Read your mind, I will." Janine wasn't impressed.

"I'm a forty-something-year-old woman, Oliver. It's called intuition. And by this age, women know to listen when the bell goes off. It's warned us on some doozies by now, and we've had to learn the hard way what happens when we ignore it. So now, even when the little tinkle bell sounds, we pay attention. Let me use my powers for some good." She smiled slyly, wiggling her fingers in the air. "Hit me with it!"

"I hope I'm way off base with this. Because if not, it's going to cause very big problems in my personal life." I thought about it again. "Yeah, very big."

Janine smacked the table in front of her, making me jump from the startling sound. "Tell me, Oliver!"

"Okay! Bailey said something strange, not out of the blue, necessarily. She'd just told me she worked at city hall and that she thought Skye was very 'ambitious,' I think is the word she used. I agreed with her, because Skye has always been extremely driven when it came to her career. Always. And the conversation wasn't a bash session. We were just talking."

"Don't give me so much fluff. Just tell me the words and let me make of it what I will. You're trying to sway me in a certain direction. And that, in itself, should be telling you something. Go on."

"I think I'm making too much of nothing. I probably shouldn't have said anything in the first place. I feel stupid for bringing it up at all." I was deeply considering just not saying another word.

"Oh no you don't. Out with it. And whatever is going on, you've already decided in your head it makes Bailey look bad and you don't want to tell me. Let me be the judge, and trust that I will give it to you straight. That's what you asked me to do, right? And I've never been anything but completely honest with you, Oliver. Now do me the same courtesy."

She had a valid point, and I really could use an outside opinion on the whole thing. So I spilled it.

"Bailey said, with reference to Skye, something along the lines of, 'sometimes being very focused on a particular goal can make you miss what's going on right in front of you' or something like that. I'm totally paraphrasing, obviously. But I've been racking my brain trying to figure out what that means."

"Did you ask her what it meant?" Janine quizzed.

"Yes, and she said it meant nothing in particular. Something about it being a general comment about the nature of the political arena. That people had to find their own way. It was all very vague. But I felt like it really did mean more. And I still do. If she was trying to give me some sort of message to warn Skye about something at work and I don't figure out what it means...and then something bad happens to Skye... How will I live with that?"

"All right," she interrupted before I could go on any longer. "Now you're just sounding dramatic. Let's look at this logically. They work in the mayor's office. The city manager's to be specific, right? We're not talking about the President of the United States here. Shit, we aren't even talking about state-level government. How deep and dark and sinister can her message have been?" Janine had a point but at the same time might have been oversimplifying the situation.

"I see what you're saying, but Skye told me some things when we were at the hospital when Hardin was at death's door."

"Really? Like what?" She sat forward on the edge of her seat again.

"She said Bailey was the puppet master behind his entire career. She had been driving him since they were in college."

"Again, Oliver, he was the city manager, not the sitting president of the free world. You're talking about them like they were Hillary and Bill. Let's not get carried away." She waved her hand dismissively. "It all just seems so over-the-top, you know?"

"You have to realize, governing a city the size of Los

Angeles is bigger business than governing some entire states." I held my hand up to stop her before she pointed out the difference. "I know what you're going to say, but this is still a big deal. We aren't talking about the town I grew up in in Iowa."

I walked over to the kitchen to grab a bottle of water from the fridge. "Anyway, the point of me telling you that was to point out Bailey is just as driven as Skye. I have to wonder if she doesn't have a hidden motive. I mean, it's possible, right?"

I sat back down, twisted the cap off the bottle, and drank about half in one gulp. "I've seen sides of both women now that honestly I'd be happy to never see again. Skye outright told me that Bailey is friends with the mayor. The mayor appoints the city manager. Since William died, they will be appointing someone to replace him until the election takes place in November, when the mayor happens to be up for re-election. But if a new mayor gets in office, who knows what will happen. Skye was banking on Bailey putting in a good word for her now so she could take the office and do a bang-up job, so whoever wins the race in November will see she's more than qualified for the job and keep her on as city manager." I knocked the cap back and forth between my fingers to expend my nervous energy.

"And that would make sense because it would be one less thing either person, the reelected mayor or a brand-new mayor, would have to deal with when starting his term." She sat back in her chair and sighed. "Well, it seems like you're really stuck between a rock and a hard place. Or have the potential to be."

"That's what I'm afraid of. I don't want to lose my best friend if I know something I should be warning her about, or if my girlfriend is gunning for her behind her back, I feel like I should warn her. Skye and I have been friends for the better part of a decade. She stood by me when even my own parents turned their backs. I can't betray her."

"But?" my business partner supplied.

"But I'm in love with Bailey. There. I said it. I love her. I want the chance to see where things can go between us. I've never felt a connection like I have with her. If Skye is manipulating me, or Bailey, in order to get what she wants, or in order to get ahead in her career, it will devastate me. Not to mention infuriate me. And I'm not convinced she's above doing that anymore. Not after the way I've seen her behave lately. She's turned a new leaf, and every once in a while, when her very practiced guard slips, I get a glimpse of it. And let me tell you, it's not pretty. If she hurts Bailey, I don't think I will be able to forgive her."

"This is quite the pickle, isn't it? Now don't hate me for saying this, but from what you've said, it sounds like Bailey has a bit of a nasty streak too. She can probably handle herself where your roommate is concerned. Especially if she's been the puppeteer to her deceased husband for all these years. Maybe you should just stay out of it and let them do their thing and see where the pieces fall."

"But no matter how it all ends, someone I really care about is going to get hurt. It's hard to sit by and watch that happen. And who's to say if I don't intervene, I won't be blamed for not stepping in when I could've helped? When I *should've* helped?"

"I think, at least for right now, you need to try your best

to concentrate on BBI. It needs all your effort to get off the ground and to do it in a strong way. All this drama with the ladies in your life is going to go on with or without you babysitting it. You're trying to apply virtue to a seemingly unethical situation. I'm not saying don't do your due diligence. Obviously, you care about them both a great deal, and you have a lot at stake too. But where are you going to be left if you only concentrate on them and not put any energy into you and your own endeavors? And I'm not just saying that because I recently sank a buttload of money into this operation, although that is derailing my train of thought marginally."

"I hear you, I do." And I had an abundance of appreciation for Janine's honesty.

"You came up with this idea, Oliver. And it's a great one. The need is there. The clients are there. Bring the service to the people. It's the only part of the equation missing. It's right there for the taking. We're this close." She held up her thumb and index finger with just a small space open between the two. "This close."

"You're right. You're exactly right. Now enough about the drama mamas. Tell me what happened with the interviews. How did we end up with only three candidates?"

Janine and I spent the next few hours digging in on ways to bulk up the stable for Book Boyfriend Inc. By the time she finished explaining how each interview went, I understood why she'd only chosen the three she had. We ended our workday with phone calls to the candidates offering them positions with BBI, and all three accepted. We planned an orientation meeting for the end of the week.

I was completely exhausted by the time she left and decided a nap was just what the doctor ordered. By the time Skye came home from work, the sun had long gone over the horizon and an autumn chill came in with her when she opened the front door.

I sat up and stretched, getting the kinks out from being curled up on the sofa.

"Must be nice." Maybe it was her attitude that chilled the air and not the outside breeze after all.

"What's that? No, never mind. How was your day?" I could be the bigger one.

"I said it must be nice. Lounging around all day," she fired back.

"Well, if I owe you any type of explanation, I was taking a nap for"—I looked at my phone—"about forty minutes. Janine and I worked for the better part of the day. We hired three new employees, oh, and a web designer. How about a glass of wine? You seem tense."

"Do I?" she asked.

I stopped on my way to the kitchen and turned to face her. "What's up?"

"With what?"

"With you? Specifically, the attitude. You seem to have a really big chip on your shoulder lately, and I seem to take the brunt of it. We've been best friends for a really long time, and I can't think of a single time you've treated me this way. So, what gives?" Honestly, I'd had all I could take of it too.

"I think you're imagining things, Oliver. Maybe you're spending too much time in these fictional worlds. You want everything to be so dramatic." She tapped on the cover of one of the romance novels Janine had left sitting on the breakfast bar. Her tone was so elitist it made my skin crawl. Nothing like the woman I once knew and loved. But how could she have made such a drastic change in such a short time?

I poured two glasses of Chardonnay and sat at the breakfast bar. I pushed one toward her by the long stem of the glass. "Tell me what's going on. I know something's up. You're not yourself. And I'm not the enemy. I'm your best friend, Skye."

"Are you? Are you, Oliver?" She sounded like a schoolgirl in a recess argument over whose turn it was to jump rope.

"Yes. Why would you even ask me that?" I was trying desperately not to rise to her bait.

"What if you're sleeping with the enemy? Does that still make you my best friend? How do I trust you then? How do I live under the same roof with you even?" She glared at me over the rim of the glass while she gulped down the wine, her hand trembling as she held the stemware.

"What the hell are you talking about? Tell me what's going on. Seriously, Skye. Tell me." Okay. This was way bigger than jump rope. Clearly.

"I think your *girlfriend* is trying to sabotage me. Everything I've worked for. All of it. Down the drain. I'll be back to fucking interning by the end of the election cycle if she gets her evil fucking way."

"Are you—"

"Don't even fucking defend her right now, Oliver. I can't bear to hear it. Not from you. That's why I haven't said anything.

That's why I've been doing my best to avoid you. I didn't want to have this little chat. But you kept pushing. You don't know that woman. Not even a little bit. She's manipulative. Calculating. Driven and unrelenting. She will stop at nothing to advance her agenda. *Nothing*."

"Sound familiar?" I said, getting oh-so-tired of this talk track.

"How dare you? Fuck you. Seriously, Oliver. You asked me what was wrong. What I was so bothered by. Asked me to tell you! You played the best friend card! And *that's* what you say to me? Just fuck off." Her eyes were welling up with tears, and I knew she was furious. I could count on one hand the number of times I'd seen Skye Delaney shed tears.

She hurried to her room and slammed the door. I even heard the little lock on the handle click into place. The silence that followed seemed louder than practice shots at a firing range. But the damage to my heart felt about the same as the barrage of holes on the humanlike paper silhouettes that were called forth and taken home as trophies, proving the marksman's accuracy at destruction. Turned out my roommate was firing with sniper-level precision.

Coincidentally, my phone chimed with a text from Bailey within five minutes. An ominous four words lit up the screen.

We need to talk.

I quickly wrote back.

Is this about Skye?

How did you know?

We just had a blowout. Again.

Spend the night?

Be there ASAP. XO

I can pick you up.

Even better.

I struggled with leaving my condo. I wanted to spend the night with Bailey, but I felt like Skye and I were at a crossroads. If I left, it would be fairly obvious where I had gone. I hadn't hung out with guy friends in months. Why would I start that night? Skye would know I wasn't home in the morning when she left to go to the office, and she would take that as a declaration of where my loyalties lay.

The whole mess seemed ridiculous when I thought about it outside of an argument or conversation, but when I got into it with her, it spun out of control so quickly because she was so emotionally charged about the topic. It seemed as though she was completely incapable of seeing reason.

It would take Bailey at least twenty minutes to get to our condo, so I thought I'd give making peace with my best friend one more try. I knocked softly on her door, hoping she had calmed down.

"Go away, Oliver," she called from inside her room.

"No, Skye, come on. I really want to talk this out. I don't want you to be mad at me."

"I'm not mad. I'm hurt." Damn, that was as bad as the famous "I'm not mad, I'm disappointed" line my mom used to throw at me to lay on the guilt. Good news! It still worked!

"I don't want to hurt you. Ever," I said to the wood grain of her bedroom door.

"I would've believed that four months ago. Shit, three months ago, even."

"Then why not now? What's changed between us? Open up, Skye. This is silly talking through the door like this." I tried the knob again, knowing damn well it was still locked.

"No. I don't want to look at you." She sounded like a petulant child.

"That's not very nice," I reprimanded. If she wanted to act like the child, I'd be the parent.

"Well, I'm not a very nice person. Not anymore."

"Don't say that." *Although it may be true.*

"Why not? It's true. Nice guys finish last. You know that's a saying for a reason, don't you?" Still sassy words, but her volume had settled to a normal level at least.

"But who are you in a race with? Who are you so worried about beating, Skye? Open the door so we can talk."

"Your girlfriend. Duh, Oliver. Are you really that dense?"

"Don't be rude on top of it. There is no race between the two of you. What are you talking about? You don't have the same job. Her husband is dead, so he's not in your way anymore. Seriously, what is all this about? Open the fucking door and talk to me!" My anger was getting the best of me, and I ended the sentence much louder than I intended.

The door flew open, bouncing off the wall when it whipped past where she stood in the doorway. "She's gunning for my job all of a sudden! Out of nowhere, she has a keen interest in city management." She paused to gloat. "I see by the confused look on your face, it's news to you too. Ask her about it." She paused again, gaining more sass as she did. "Oh, wait, maybe she'll lie to you too like she's been lying to me all this time! She's a lying bitch, Oliver! Telling me she was going to recommend me to the mayor, her old friend. Old friend, my ass! She's probably been sucking his dick in the staff lounge on her lunch break! They seem awfully cozy for old friends."

My voice dropped an octave in warning. "Shut your fucking mouth right now. You're so over the line it's not even funny."

"Ooops. Sorry. Was she sucking your dick last night? Then his today? Too much to unsee in your mind right now? Sorry?" She shrugged impishly. "Not sorry! *Bestie.*"

My temper snapped, and I fired back. "Holy fuck, you've become a raving-mad bitch! What has gotten into you? Is this all over a job? I don't think I like you very much right now. You know what? I'm going to go wait outside. For my girlfriend, who's picking me up to spend the night at her house. Where she'll likely be sucking my dick! Again! Thank you very much."

When she went to speak, I stopped her. "Don't say another fucking word. I *love* her." When her mouth fell open in disbelief, I continued, "You heard me. I've fallen in love with her. If you want to salvage our friendship at all from this point, you need to think long and hard about whatever the fuck is going on in that crazy head of yours and get your shit together. And before you even consider speaking to me again, make sure you start with the words, 'Oliver, I owe you an apology.'"

Leaving her standing in the doorway of her room, I turned on my heel and walked out. I grabbed my backpack off the back of the sofa and went out the front door, slamming it so hard, the windows shook in our condo and the neighbors'. Bailey pulled up just as I got to the curb, and I was never happier to see someone in my life.

"Drive. Just drive. I'd be happy to never come back here again," I muttered in the darkened car as we sped off into the night.

CHAPTER TWELVE

"Oh my God. No more. Seriously. What's gotten into you? I mean, I'm not *actually* complaining, but I may not be able to walk tomorrow if you come near me one more time." Bailey rolled over onto her back, sweat-matted hair stuck to her forehead in little ringlets.

I lay back against the pillows and grinned. I'd felt possessed since we'd gotten back to her house. Literally not able to get my fill of her. My arms already felt empty without her in them, so I tugged her closer, and she willingly scooted to my side in the giant bed. She had told me that she and her deceased husband had never slept in that room together, and that he slept in the guest area of the house because he usually worked late or went to social functions and came in late, so it didn't feel odd to be intimate with her here.

"What happened tonight?" she asked.

"Hmmm? I'd say we rocked the house down, wouldn't you?" I looked down to where she toyed with the hills and valleys of my abs.

"No, I mean with Skye. You were really angry when I picked you up. Told me to never take you back."

"Oh, that."

"Yeah. That."

"Can we not talk about it? I just want to be here with you. In this moment. So much better. Happier." Thinking about that clusterfuck ruined my mellow mood instantly.

"Sure. But whatever it is, it doesn't sound like it's going to go away by ignoring it."

"No, you're right. It's not. So just putting it on the back burner until morning isn't going to matter much. You know? It's still going to be right there when we wake up."

"Okay. You have a point. And it's already late. And there's no way I can be late again tomorrow. We can talk in the morning." She pulled the covers up over both of us and snuggled into my side.

◆ ◆ ◆ ◆

The sun shone through the French doors much sooner than either of us would have preferred. We had both slept through the night, barely moving other than an occasional readjustment here or there.

"You shower, I'll get us some coffee," I offered, knowing her routine would be much longer than mine. I grabbed my phone off the nightstand to check email while the coffee brewed. Several messages went straight into the trash folder unopened. No matter how often I unsubscribed from certain mailing lists, the messages continued to show up in my inbox each morning. The first legitimate email to catch my eye was from the property-management company of the condo complex where Skye and I rented our place. Our lease was coming up for renewal, and in addition to the rent going up slightly, they wanted us to sign a longer lease than we had previously. A quick scan of the addressees confirmed Skye had also received the email. It would be interesting to see if she would call me to discuss how we would handle the situation.

With two steaming cups of Colombian perfection in hand, I returned to the master bathroom just in time to watch my glorious girlfriend step out of the shower, tiny beads of water running down her neck and chest to be absorbed by the bountiful white towel wrapped securely around her torso. All signs of my name had disappeared from her otherwise flawless skin, and a bit of sadness passed through my heart because of it. I really did enjoy seeing the outward sign of our evening's activities.

"See if this is the way you like it." I handed her the mug, hoping I had her java preferences memorized properly.

After taking a careful sip, she grinned. "How did you know how I like my coffee? I don't think my husband would've known on the day he passed away. I'm not trying to be disrespectful to his memory. I'm just saying, I don't think he ever took the time to learn the big things about me, let alone the small things like cream and sugar."

"I care about you. I want to learn everything about you, Bailey. The big things, the little things, and everything in between. I want to know if you like rainstorms or snowstorms. If you have a nightmare, I want to hold you until you fall back to sleep. If you have a great day at work and have reason to celebrate, I want to pour the champagne. There's so much to experience in life; I want to do it with you."

"You're such a poet, Oliver. And so early in the morning." She looked at me sideways, almost as though she didn't trust my words.

"I'm serious, Bailey." I took her coffee from her hands and set it on the counter. When she stared at me, her giant emerald eyes getting wider with curiosity, I put her hands up to my lips and kissed her knuckles. I had to tell her how I felt, and right then was as good of a time as any.

"I'm falling in love with you."

She stared up at me, eyes filling with tears. One fat drop spilled over and ran down her cheek.

"I don't think I expected you to cry. I'm not sure what to do with that." I laughed, but it was nerves getting the better of me.

"And I don't think I expected you to say that you were falling in love with me this morning."

"Does it bother you? That I feel that way? That I said I love you?"

"No." Another tear trickled down her cheek while she shook her head.

"Then why are you crying? Tell me what's wrong."

"I don't know what to say. I don't know... I just don't know. My life is so... I'm so... I'm not sure of the right word? Afraid? I feel like I don't know myself right now. Maybe? I lived so long being William's wife, and he and I were never really *in* love, you know? I mean, we loved one another. But we weren't in love. What if I don't know *how* to be in love?"

"I don't think it's something you necessarily have to know how to do. I think you just follow your heart."

"I'm not sure mine works properly, though. It doesn't seem to follow the conventional ideals. And...you," she stammered. "I mean look at you." She waved her hand up and down in front of my body before swiping another tear from her cheek.

I looked down the length of my body to my toes and then up again, missing what she was pointing out. "I don't understand."

"You're so romantic—so charming and good at all this courting and thoughtfulness. I'm really worried I'll just disappoint you. I'll never measure up."

"Baby. You're being ridiculous. The things I do for you? I do because I want to. I want to make you happy—bring a little smile to your face during the day—make you think of me and make your heart flutter. That's all." I shrugged. "It doesn't take much more than a little thoughtfulness."

"Like I said, I think it just scares me. I'm out of my element here because it's unfamiliar territory."

"I understand that. I can only hope that you think I'm worth giving love a try. Like a real shot at love. The way it's supposed to be, not just a relationship of convenience for the sake of someone's career." After I'd said it, I hoped I hadn't gone too far. But she'd admitted, in not so many words, that's all her marriage to William had been.

"Let's take it one day at a time. The way life is meant to be lived. Instead of a grand plan and a well-laid-out scheme. That's the way I lived my life before, and I would really like a break from that. I'm going to admit something to you that I never admitted to anyone else. When William died, I was relieved. I know that sounds horrible. And you may judge me for saying that on some level. But he and I had had our whole lives planned out since we were in college. We had the whole thing thought through, year by year, what we should be doing, where we should be career-wise, where we should be living, who we should be friends with, who we should know professionally. You name it, it was planned in advance." She sat down on the bench in front of her vanity mirror.

"When he passed, I let all of that go. And it felt fabulous. The strain, the constant pressure, it was daunting. I mean, can you imagine that?" She looked sideways at me to get my input. "I wonder how much of that stress led to his heart attack. Well, that and the drugs and drinking. But the public will never know any of that either. Boy, I'm just spilling all kinds of secrets this morning, aren't I?"

I squatted down in front of her, gripping her knees to steady myself and have physical contact while I spoke. "You can trust me. You can count on me as well. I won't let you down or betray you. Okay? The only thing I can do to prove that to you is give you my time. Time doing exactly what I say I will do."

"You're a good man, Oliver Connely. I fear almost too good to be true." She leaned forward and pressed her forehead to mine. "I don't want to break up all of this bonding time, but I cannot be late for work this morning. Very important things are going on around the office, and I need to be sure I'm there on time or it will look bad. Very bad."

"I understand." I stood up and started stripping on my way over to the shower stall. "But that brings us to another less pleasant subject. Skye. She was acting straight-up crazy last night. Saying ridiculous things about you wanting to be the city manager now. What is she going on about? And what exactly do you do now?" I figured the best way to get straight answers was to ask straight questions.

"Well, she's not being all that crazy, but she doesn't understand the motive. I'm trying to do her a favor, and no matter what I say, she's going to believe what she's going to believe. I currently work as a clerk in the finance director's office. It's a dead-end position, but it keeps me busy, and it kept me in the mix when William was the city manager, so I always knew all the players in the game."

"Is there something I could tell her that would ease her suspicions? You should've heard her last night." I shook my head, remembering. "She was downright vicious, and I fear she's going to do something rash if she doesn't have her fears laid to rest somehow." I thought about our fight last night for a second. "The more I think about it, I don't know if she'd even listen to me right now. We parted on a pretty sour note."

"Like I said, probably anything I tell you will fall on deaf ears with Skye now. She has her mind made up, and until all the pieces of the puzzle fall into place, neither you nor I will be able to tell her differently. I warned you before that she is her own worst enemy. She's focused on the end goal and missing what's going on in front of her. It happens to a lot of career-minded people. Especially in politics. And, unfortunately, many people who have been in the game for a long time know that it's a common pitfall of the younger, hungry staffers and aides, so they use them to their advantage."

Bailey disappeared into her walk-in closet for several minutes to get dressed. I finished showering and was dried off and half-dressed when she emerged in a tailored navy suit, ivory blouse that had a loose tie at the keyhole neckline, and navy-and-ivory spectator pumps in her grip by the heels.

"Are you almost ready? I can drop you off wherever you need to be on my way downtown," she offered.

"No, that's okay. I can catch an Uber from here if you don't mind me locking up."

"You know what? I don't know why I didn't think of this before. I have an SUV just sitting in the garage, not being used. Why don't you take that? I'm sure it would do it some good to be driven."

"No, I don't want to impose like that."

"You're not imposing. You'd be doing me a favor. And look, if we're going to be doing this whole love thing, then we share our stuff, right?"

I grinned so big, my face felt like it would split in half. "Right."

She came closer, stood on her tiptoes, and kissed me. "I need to go. The keys are on the hook by the back door. It's the BMW key ring. There's a house key on there too. Just press 'arm' and then 'away' when you go out and lock the door. The garage is detached out back. By the gate you came in the other night." She kissed me again, but this time I wrapped my arms around her waist and really kissed her deeply. I was so happy she was signing on for an all-in relationship. I planned on doing everything in my power to make sure she wouldn't regret it.

"All right. I'll talk to you later. Go. Play nice at recess." I watched her walk out of the bedroom and listened as she clip-clopped across the hardwood floor downstairs after putting on her heels. I even waited to hear her go out the back door and heard the sound of her sexy little sports car start up in the garage out back and then finally finished getting ready when I heard her speed off down the quiet suburban block.

Life was good. Life was really good, and I wanted it to stay that way. I needed to figure out how to deal with Skye and her irrational paranoia about Bailey. I didn't want to have to choose between the two most important people in my life, but Skye was making it seem like that was the only way she would have it.

Something struck me as I was backing the X5 out of the spotless garage behind the house. Bailey never outright denied Skye's accusation. I'd told her that my best friend said she thought she was gunning for the city manager's job, but Bailey never denied that she was. She only said until all the pieces came together, Skye wouldn't believe that Bailey was trying to help her, not sabotage her. And I had to agree with Bailey... If I took any of that information to Skye, it would just enrage her more. When people were extremely driven, like Skye was, everyone else seemed like they were out to get them, hurt their cause, or stand in their way. They were convinced the world wanted to see them fail. I didn't know what was making her feel that way specifically, but according to Bailey, if she wasn't careful, it was going to be her undoing.

Burying myself in Book Boyfriend Inc. was the only way not to get consumed with worry for the women in my life. There was plenty to do while getting a new company off the ground. Janine spent a few hours coaching the new hires on the finer points of acting like gentlemen. It had turned out to be the breaking point for the candidates who didn't make the cut in the first round of the interviews. Janine was horrified at their table manners and general lack of civility when it came to treating their dates like ladies. She'd said, and probably rightly so, that our clients would end up demanding their money back if we sent them on dates with a couple of the guys she had interviewed.

Learning the accounting software she loaded onto my laptop that morning when she came over was proving to be an even bigger challenge. It was confusing and simple at the same time. Everything seemed very obvious once she explained it, and I felt like I was doing nothing but frustrating her with my questions. Maybe hiring someone to do the books was a better idea than trying to do them myself. But we needed to mind the budget while we got up and running, so I had to do as much as I could myself. I looked at the chart of accounts one more time, trying to understand why it was set up the way it was.

The day flew by, and before I knew it, Janine was packing her stuff up and heading home. Which meant Skye would be home any minute too. I considered doing the cowardly thing and leaving, but no sooner had Janine cleared the front sidewalk than Little Mary Sunshine came barreling through the door, hair pulled back in a severe bun, cheeks red from the late-day sun. Or at least I thought.

Once she was inside and took off her sunglasses, I saw she was crying.

"Hey, what's going on? You okay?" I loved Skye, and my concern was genuine.

"Do. Not. Speak. To. Me."

I just stared at her. Whatever was going on, I wasn't sure I wanted to be involved, judging by the tone of her voice.

"Aren't you going to say anything?" she challenged.

"You just told me not to. I can't keep up with you, Skye."

"She fucking got my job! Are you happy now?"

"Who did? What job? What are you talking about?" Honestly, I was trying to keep up. I was pretty sure she was talking about Bailey, but Bailey had told me just that morning she worked in the finance director's office.

"Your sugar mama. My job. The job she was supposed to help me get! Remember all that? Don't play fucking dumb with me, Oliver! It doesn't suit you!"

"You need to stop this nonsense." I shook my head, attempting to walk away from her. But she grabbed my arm.

"It's not nonsense! How does a no one come from nowhere and take a job they know nothing about? It makes zero sense! Everyone in the entire office is whispering about her now. Convinced she's sleeping with the mayor or sucking him off or something! Maybe she has serious dirt on him. I don't know, but none of it makes sense!" Little bits of spittle had collected in the corners of her mouth from her hysterical shouting.

"Maybe there's more—"

"Do not defend her!"

"Well, someone has to! Do you expect me to sit here and listen to you rail on her over and over? I won't do it, Skye." I had had enough.

"Not even for your best friend? Not even then, Oliver? You're trading a piece of ass for your best friend? I can't take it anymore. I want you out of this house." She folded her arms across her chest in defiance.

"That's fine. When you come to your senses, let me know."

"No, I mean for good. Take your things and go. I know you got the lease renewal. I won't be signing it with you. You can take your things and go. Make other arrangements. Our lease, like our friendship, is over."

"Skye...don't be like this..."

"Goodbye, Oliver."

Then she went into her room and closed the door. The patented Skye Delaney kiss-off. I knew, above all else, she did "you're dead to me" better than anyone I'd ever seen. When she said it, she meant it.

A quick text to Bailey let her know I'd be coming over late. It was going to take a while to pack up my stuff. Even though we had until the end of the month on our current lease, I didn't want to be in the condo any longer than I needed to be. I could get a lot done that night and finish the rest the following day. Strangely, Bailey didn't mention a single word about work drama while we were texting.

Another message went out to Janine letting her know we'd need a new place for base camp for BBI. She offered her place, but I said I'd rather not be in the complex at all, that way I wouldn't chance running into Skye. She said she had another property we might be able to use, and she would get back to me by the morning. She and I were going to have to really go over the finances closely so I could determine how much I could afford to pay in rent. I would probably need to find a roommate again, and the whole idea pissed me off. Skye and I had had such an easy living arrangement worked out for so long; starting all over with someone else was going to suck.

I was exhausted by the time I pulled back into the garage

behind Bailey's house. She stood at the back door, waiting for me as I came up the walk, a dusty-pink silk robe skimming the middle of her thighs.

"You are a vision for my weary eyes." I nuzzled between her breasts from the bottom step while she stood just inside the back door, putting her at the perfect height for my face to rest on her chest.

"I thought you sounded like you needed a little extra TLC when we talked. I ran a bath upstairs."

"Are you for real? Am I dreaming? Please don't wake me if I am." I kissed her thoroughly, not wanting to stop when she pulled away.

"I think I'm the one who doesn't ever want to wake up. Come on. Let me take care of you for a change." She pulled me by the hand, all the way upstairs to her master suite, and undressed me in front of her ridiculously large garden tub before dropping her own robe and getting in.

We took turns washing each other, lathering and buffing each other's body. Until the water was too cool to be enjoyable, we stayed in the tub and talked about everything under the sun, except the enormous elephant in the room.

While we dried off and got ready for bed, I finally broke down and asked her what had happened at the office.

"It would be better if you didn't get involved, Oliver."

"I think it's too late for that. Skye dragged me right into the middle of it this afternoon."

"Is that what led to the abrupt packing?" she asked before starting to brush her teeth.

"Kind of. Well, yes, actually. Although, I think that was

in the cards, no matter what. We both got an email from our landlord that our rent was going up and they wanted us to sign a longer lease. But after whatever happened at the office today, she said I was clearly choosing you over her and she never wanted to see me again."

She rinsed and said, "That seems a bit extreme, no? And, frankly, immature. Why is she making you a part of all of this?"

"Skye is a very loyal friend. She expects the same in return."

"But you've been nothing but loyal as well." Her defense of me was endearing.

"Apparently, she sees it differently."

"I'm sorry about all of this. I feel terrible."

"Just tell me what's going on. At least then I'll understand why my best friend hates me." I took my turn at brushing while she explained.

"The mayor appointed me to my deceased husband's job today. It's just until the election is held in November. That's less than two months away. He thinks I'm qualified, which I am, and he thinks I know what projects William was working on when he passed, which I do. He thinks I know the relationships William had built with key members of the city, which I do. In theory, it makes perfect sense for me to fill the position in the interim. However, the go-getters who want the job permanently are very upset at the moment. Skye is one of those people. And that is understandable as well. But, as I've explained to you before, there are reasons things happen the way they do. And sometimes, trusting the process is the hardest part of any experience. That is a life lesson that is best learned early, and with grace and gratitude, neither of which your best friend is exemplifying at the moment."

We both finished in the bathroom and moved toward the bedroom.

"Former best friend," I added dryly.

"I'm sorry about that, Oliver. I hope she'll come around when the dust settles. I have a pretty good feeling she will. As long as you keep the light on."

"I'm not following." I looked at her quizzically.

"Well, I mean as long as you're open to forgiving her. She may need a good friend in the months to come. You once told me that she was there for you when no one else was. She may need you to return that favor. So maybe don't write her out of your story just yet." She pulled the covers back on her side of the bed, and I did the same.

"You amaze me, you know that?" I watched her while I climbed onto the thick mattress, letting the weight of the day sink into the memory foam.

"Why do you say that? I just told you I took your best friend's job out from under her nose, in turn causing her to kick you out of your house and declare you excommunicated, and you say I amaze you?" She got in and pulled the covers up to her chin.

"But then you went on to hint at some cosmic reason for things happening the way they do and that my very rude and nasty best friend—pardon me, former best friend—just may need a shoulder to cry on in the near future and I should keep a box of tissues at the ready. I see that as amazing." I kissed the tip of her nose as we lay facing one another, huddled under the covers.

"I have an idea. I want you to really think about it, though, before you say no. Okay?" She looked like a little girl as excitement lit up her eyes.

"Okay."

"What would you think about moving in here with me?"

I opened my mouth to answer and then closed it. My knee-jerk reaction was to immediately say yes, but I didn't want to seem overenthusiastic. And Skye's rude comment about Bailey being my sugar mama came to mind. It was the last thing I wanted people to think of our relationship.

"Okay, I'll think about it." She looked deflated when I gave my response. "Hey, I just don't want you to be making an offer because you're feeling bad about what went on with Skye tonight. I want you to be sure it's what you want too." I felt impressed for thinking so quickly on my feet.

"Trust me. I'm very sure. I wouldn't have made the offer otherwise."

"Well, let's give it a couple of days, and then we can talk about it again. Let's say, by the end of the week, when I need to be out of the condo? Then I will know where I'm moving my stuff to. Deal?" I offered.

"Don't feel pressured."

"I don't. I want you to know that I'd love to live here with you. But I want to give you a little more time to really think about it."

"I already said I have. I've fantasized about it a lot, actually, since the first time you and I met."

"Really?" The word "fantasy" sent my mind down a whole different path. "Tell me about your fantasy. What was it like?

Did I come home like tonight and you were waiting for me?"

"Mmmm-hmmm." She sounded coy.

I slid my hand beneath the covers, searching until I found her body. I pulled her silky pajama top up and laid my palm across her stomach. Her skin was warm against mine.

"What else? Did we bother with dinner, or did we go right upstairs to bed?" I teased.

"We went to bed, always straight to bed," she whispered.

"We're smart, after all."

I moved on top of her, kissing her neck, biting her shoulder where I could pull the silky top away far enough. I sat back and unbuttoned her shirt, exposing her pert breasts to the cool air of the room. Her nipples responded by stiffening. I danced my fingers across the tight peaks, pinching lightly as her eyes fell closed. I followed with my mouth, licking and teasing the firm points until she moaned with pleasure. Resisting the urge to sink my teeth into her breast took all of my restraint. I wanted to mark her again as I had in the past.

I interrupted whatever fantasy played behind her closed lids. "Tell me what else."

"Hmmmm?" She smiled and looked up at me.

"What else happens in your dreams, baby?" I lay beside her again so I could touch all of her.

"You fuck me," she said softly, still shy with her thoughts.

"Of course I do. But tell me how."

"How?" She squirmed beside me.

"Yes. How? Is it gentle? Rough? Are you on top? From behind? Tell me about it. I want to know what you see."

"Ohhhh. Mmmmm." She sighed while I continued to

lightly make designs with my fingertips on her bare skin. Every so often, my fingers dipped beneath the waistband of her pajama bottoms but never got quite close enough to what she wanted. She started moving her hips in time with my hand, trying to guide it closer to her clit.

"Tell me, Bay." I grazed over the top of her pussy lips, so wet from the teasing. Her moans made my cock throb in my boxers, leaving a wet spot behind to torment me further.

"Roll onto your belly," I whispered in her ear, loving that she did so without the argument I would've gotten only months ago when we first started dating. Moving behind her, I rubbed her ass cheeks roughly with the palms of my hand, in turn grinding her pelvis into the mattress.

"That feels sooooo good, Oliver," she mumbled into the bedding.

"Good, baby. Tell me. Tell me what feels good for you. Tell me what you want from me, and it's yours. I'm yours, Bailey."

I leaned over her body and kissed down her shoulder, moving her hair off to one side and continuing a trail of wet kisses down the center of her back, nipping at her flesh in different spots. Sometimes harder than others, sometimes just light kisses.

"Spread your legs, baby." She moved her thighs apart by about four inches, just enough space to fit my hand between them. "That's good. Let me feel you." I teased her lightly, knowing if she wanted more she would have to willingly spread her legs farther, and knowing if she did that for me, it would do something to the animal inside me. Watching a woman spread her legs for you, as a man, was one of the sexiest fucking sights of human existence. I continued taunting her clit and pussy until she was soaked and just about crazed with the need to come.

"Please, Oliver. Please. I can't take much more."

"I know, gorgeous. You're so swollen. So ready."

"God. Do it. Please. Or I can finish it if you don't want to. Please, one way or the other. I'm going crazy." She raised her ass in the air like a good girl and spread her legs for me, and I nearly came at the sight.

"Christ, Bailey. So fucking sexy. Do you want me to fuck you?"

"Yes! God, yes!"

I reached under her waist with my forearm and hoisted her weight up off the bed so she was up on her hands and knees, and then I drove into her, all in one swift motion. I kept her steady with my arm while I pounded into her, over and over, driven by the sight of her wet cunt, hungry and wrapped around my cock.

"Tell me now, baby. What happened in your fantasy at this part? Did you come like a good girl?"

"Yes! Oh my God, Oliver. Yes! Every time with you, I do. So good. Oh, yes! Yes!" She buried her face in the pillow and let out such a howl, I worried that I was hurting her. But when I felt her gripping my cock with her release, I mentally added the sound to the epic orgasm playlist.

I followed right behind with my own animal-like sound, releasing my load into her pussy, which was still milking me with the aftershocks of her orgasm. "Holy shit, woman. You're killing me. One orgasm at a time. Killing me." I leaned over her back and rested my head between her shoulders until her arms and legs gave out and we fell flat to the mattress. I pulled her close to me as we rolled to our sides, fluid leaking from both of us.

"I like your fantasy, baby. Good stuff."

"You're always the star," she said with a yawn.

"You make it easy to find inspiration." I kissed the back of her head.

"I didn't tell you about the last part, though. You may change your mind." She said it so quietly, I wasn't sure if I heard her right.

"Uh-oh. Should I ask? Maybe not. Maybe we should just go to sleep. I'm not ever going to be into sharing you or anything like that. So if that's it, yeah, don't tell me. Let's just go to sleep."

"That's not it." She laughed lightly, turning onto her back.

"Okay. Cool. Anything else I can handle." I twisted our hands together and rested them on top of her stomach.

But she just lay there quietly.

"Well, are you going to tell me?"

Still, she stayed quiet.

"Do I have to tickle it out of you?" I dug my fingers into her ribs, and she burst into giggles.

"Okay! Okay! I'll tell you. I hate being tickled. Always have."

She just stared up into my eyes. She was really weighing the pros and cons of telling me, whatever it was.

"Just say it. I'm dying of curiosity now," I urged her.

"In my fantasy, you and I..."

I waited for the bomb to drop. The way she was building up to it, it was going to be a doozy.

"Have a baby," she whispered.

Boom! Hiroshima! Pearl Harbor and Nagasaki all at the same time.

Pulling her closer, I buried my nose in her hair. "You have a very active imagination. Can I ask why you haven't had any children up to this point?"

"Well, there are a couple reasons, really. William never wanted children. He wasn't fond of them at any stage, and it was a dream I gave up for him. And then, it turned out he was sterile, or at least that's what he told me. When he passed, the autopsy report said that he'd had a vasectomy. So, he'd actually lied to me and had had an elective procedure to prevent us from ever having children. That really hurt me. I suppose it was for the better, seeing how often he was sleeping with other women. But still, he knew how badly I wanted a baby."

I tugged on her shoulder so she would turn and face me. "That's horrible. That was horrible of him to do that to you. I'm sorry you had to find out that way. I'm sorry you had to find out at all." I pulled her into my embrace and held her there for a few minutes. I still felt like I needed to address the topic as it pertained to us, though. I leaned back a bit so I could see her face while I spoke. "I never really gave having children much thought. I always figured that was something I would think about later in my life, you know?"

"Do you *want* to have children?"

"I've always said I'd like to be a father. Someday."

"I think that's enough to work with. It's important to me.

I just know I don't want to be in another relationship with someone who doesn't want a family. If I'm going to have a chance at a do-over, I'm going to do it the exact way I want to do it."

I just smiled and kissed her. I loved her conviction and her passion for life. If only the other woman I used to say those exact same things about could appreciate what I saw in her.

Because I had a fantasy of my own. I had always hoped that Skye and my wife would end up being the best of friends someday too. I had to hold out hope that things were going to work themselves out.

CHAPTER THIRTEEN

"Are you sure you can be there? It's at ten fifteen sharp. You can't be late. You have to be on time. In fact, be there early. You'll want to be there early. Can you be there early?"

"Oh my God, woman. How many cups of coffee did you have this morning?" I was driving Bailey to the office. She'd told me she had a very important press conference that morning, and she asked me to come back and be there for the event. She even made sure I wore a suit and tie.

"I'm very proud of you, baby." I squeezed her hand while I navigated through downtown rush-hour gridlock.

"What for? You don't even know what's going on. I mean, you don't, do you?" Panic crossed her face. If she wasn't already so tense, it would've been a little comical.

"No. But whatever it is, it seems very important. And I'll always be proud of you. You've been working day and night for the past three weeks, so whatever you've been doing, I'm guessing this is the culmination?"

"It is." She took a deep breath and let it out. "And it is *very* important. And I'm so glad you're going to be there." She took a turn at the hand-squeezing action. "You look gorgeous, by the way."

"Thank you. You look stunning, as always. That jade

blouse is the best with the gray suit. Great choice."

"Well, having a sexy ex-fashion model living under my roof helps for many reasons. This is one that I can talk about in public without blushing."

"Yeah? Name one reason that makes you blush?" I goaded her to tell me more.

"Oh no you don't," she teased. "I need to keep my head in the game today. Nice try, though. Tonight, on the other hand, all bets are off. Maybe tonight, you can tell me about one of *your* fantasies." She waggled her brows when I looked over at her.

"Oooooh, careful what you sign up for, girl."

"Darn! Would you look at that! We're here already!" Her smile was radiant as she gathered her things from behind the driver's-side seat, easier to reach from the front passenger seat. "Remember, ten fifteen. Make sure you're here on time. Maybe you shouldn't leave the area. Just go park and work from your laptop at the café across the street?"

"Bailey?" I had learned to interrupt her when she got neurotic.

"Hmmm?" She looked up from stuffing papers into her bag.

"Go. I got this," I said calmly, bestowing my Zen aura onto her.

"Sorry. I love you." She stretched across the console, and I kissed her.

"I love you. You're going to be awesome."

"Yeah, I am," she said with confidence.

Regardless of how annoying she was being, I took her

advice and parked in the employee parking garage, since the SUV had a permit on it, and camped out across the street at the coffee shop. I had a bunch of invoicing to do for BBI, and it was the perfect spot to hop on free Wi-Fi and get it done.

I had moved into Bailey's house three weeks ago, and so far, things were working out great. We'd found an easy rhythm around each other and were getting along like naturals. She'd been working on a big project at work, so she'd been putting in extra hours. I usually had dinner waiting for her when she got home, but she picked at her food like a bird. I was doing my best to get her to change her eating habits, but she was a stubborn mule when she wanted to be. Somehow, it made me love her even more.

I made my way to the common area in front of city hall, where press conferences were customarily held. Satellite trucks from local news channels were parked at the curb, with cameramen and television personalities milling about, waiting for the event to start. Folding chairs were lined up in neat rows in front of the wooden podium in the center of the roped-off common. I showed the security guard the press pass Bailey had given me that morning and made my way to the front to claim a seat.

Chairs filled up quickly as the time approached ten fifteen. I could see Bailey pacing inside the corridor of the building, waiting for the event to start. Clearly, she was going to be giving the press conference or at least be one of the main speakers. A few other people milled around with her inside, but she seemed to maintain a few feet of space between her and everyone else at all times. Surprisingly, Skye emerged from the building with a few of her coworkers that I recognized from various functions I had attended with her. One of the women gave me a quick wave when she saw me sitting there before remembering I was now on the enemy's team and dropped her hand in embarrassment.

As the press conference got underway, the mayor made his way to the microphone, introduced himself, the chief of police, Bailey—who was the acting city manager—the city controller, and the city attorney. It was unusual to have the top brass of the city all in one place at the same time. Eight of the fifteen members of the city council were in attendance in the front row of chairs, each standing and waving to the crowd when their names were announced. Something big was about to go down, because the gang was definitely all here.

"At this time, I'd like to turn the microphone over to the acting city manager, Bailey Hardin, who will present the State of the City address in her late husband's stead." The well-groomed man hugged Bailey when she approached, and Skye physically turned in her seat to give me an "I told you so" glare and then turned back to face forward. It was the most immature thing I'd ever seen her do in our entire friendship, and I felt both embarrassed and ashamed for her at the same time. Her jealousy and lust for power were turning her into an awful person. There was nothing remotely inappropriate about the public greeting that was exchanged between the two colleagues.

"Good morning, ladies and gentlemen, my fellow Angelinos, city officials, family members, and friends. We are gathered here this morning, under the beautiful California sun that we are so fortunate to claim as our home, under false pretenses. I'm sorry to have misled you all into thinking we came here for the State of the City address, but it was necessary to gather the officials needed to hear the charges that are about to be brought against the sitting mayor of Los Angeles and have him immediately dismissed as the leader of our fine city."

Immediately, murmurs spread through the people in attendance, and a few even shot to their feet and beelined toward the building. Bailey seemed to make eye contact with a few of the uniformed police officers stationed at the entrances before continuing with her speech. The crowd settled down quickly to hear what she would say next.

"These circumstances are unusual, indeed, and legal proceedings will take place justly, and swiftly, but behind closed doors. It was important, to me and the other officials involved, that the public know and understand the misuse of power and wrongdoing going on in city hall during Mayor Roberts's tenure.

"My husband was a corrupt man. He fit in well in this administration, and it wasn't until his untimely death that I began to uncover such wrongdoings that I just couldn't sit back, in good conscience as a citizen of this city, and watch go on. When I began investigating in the capacity of my former position in the city's financial office, I quickly uncovered alleged misappropriation of campaign funds, bribery, and gambling. We have evidence that also gives cause to investigate accusations of sexual misconduct, drug abuse, corruption of a minor, sex with a minor, and prostitution.

"Again, all accusations are alleged at this time, and the

city's district attorney's office will have their work cut out for them in the upcoming months. I worked with other officials in the mayor's office, those who you see here today"—she motioned to the people sitting in the front row, on the side of the podium opposite Skye—"that hold either appointed positions or elected offices, to gather evidence to have the mayor and several other officials relieved of their duties.

"The police chief and his officers are here today to see that no person who is being charged with a crime, whether it be felony or misdemeanor, leaves the premise before being duly processed. All of the exits are being monitored, and we appreciate everyone just staying in their seats while the police chief and his department take care of their duties. I thank you for coming out today. We won't be answering questions at this time. Thank you."

As soon as she finished speaking, she sought my face in the crowd. When our eyes met, she beamed, and I had never been so proud of another person in my entire life. She had been working so hard on this, and I knew it was something very important to her, but I'd had no idea the gravity of the situation. She was a true hero for our city. Whatever she had discovered in her husband's affairs, she had chosen not to bury it. Instead of protecting his rotten name, she had decided to bring corrupt people to justice.

A decent amount of chaos ensued. The mayor was not interested in cooperating, nor were many of the others who had just been implicated on live social media and mainstream news coverage. However, Bailey and her team had a good plan in place, and even those who escaped into the building were detained at locked exits inside. No one got out without showing proper identification and being cleared by the law enforcement officials who were stationed at every exit. Over the course of the following three hours, all but four of the accused were taken into custody. Of the missing four, two were said to still be in the building, trying to tie up loose ends in their offices, and the other two were simply unaccounted for.

As for Mayor Roberts, he was seeking private council with his attorney in the holding room of the county jail.

Leaning against the wall outside Bailey's office, I heard her hang up the phone, for what I hoped was the last time. I peeked my head around the doorjamb. "I'm taking you home. Kicking and screaming if I have to."

"I'm so ready. I'm exhausted."

"You were amazing today." I beamed, crossing the room to where she leaned against her desk.

"Thank you, Oliver." She kissed me, and I quickly grabbed her waist and pulled her closer.

"You could've told me this was going on. I could've helped. I don't know, done something..." I brushed a stray hair back behind her ear.

"I had to do it myself. I hope you understand. The more I dug, the more I found out. My heart broke every day. I don't know when it all fell apart for William. We'd planned a lot of things, but being corrupt wasn't part of those dreams. We were young and idealistic. Somewhere that turned into taking bribes, doing drugs." She shook her head, her voice cracking and then trailing off. "He was renting hookers and hotel rooms on a weekly basis, Oliver. Using taxpayer money to have sex with girls barely old enough to vote."

All I could do was hold her in my arms. What could I say in response? He was an asshole. A lying, cheating scoundrel. Skye always knew it. She told me repeatedly that he was a piece of shit. She was just biding her time until he got caught or the next election cycle passed and hoped he would be replaced.

"What happens now?" I asked.

"What do you mean?"

"Well, with you, for starters. This job. The mayor. There's going to be a lot of upheaval around here. Especially in the coming weeks."

"That's putting it mildly. The members of the city council have been working very closely with the police chief and the district attorney, trying to figure out who will be removed from office and who will be left standing. Obviously, because of his level of involvement, the mayor will be relieved. The election is now a month out. The city council will probably hold down the fort—so to speak—until then. They may have their chairman stand in as acting mayor, because it certainly won't be me.

"The only reason I accepted the appointment from the mayor in the first place was so I could get on the inside and finish getting the evidence I needed to put them all away. I've never had political aspirations of my own. I know that was hard for others around here to believe, but it's the truth.

"And as far as Skye is concerned, I was trying to save her from being associated with a scandal like this. If her name was tarnished this early in her political career, she may as well have found a new career path altogether. So, whether she ever believes it or not, I was trying to help her, not sabotage her.

The minute I realized what was going on, I switched my strategy from helping get her appointed to getting myself appointed instead." Her eyes searched mine while she spoke.

"And I will never be able to repay you."

We both turned abruptly toward the open doorway of Bailey's office, where my former best friend stood, clutching a stack of folders against her chest.

"Skye. How long have you been standing there?" Bailey asked, pulling out of my arms and standing up straight.

"Long enough. I came to give my resignation, figuring you would be appointed the mayor pro tem at minimum. Although I don't think we've had an MPT in years." She smiled. An actual smile. Looking once again like the beautiful woman I loved with all my heart.

"Maybe I should leave you two alone?" Bailey started toward the door, and Skye objected first, before I had a chance to do the same.

"No, please stay. I need to talk with both of you. Although I would like to do it privately, so would either of you mind if I close the door?" Contrite Skye was definitely not the girl I was used to seeing very often.

Bailey and I both shook our heads, and she came back and stood beside me. "Let's sit down." She motioned to the grouping of chairs just beyond her desk.

Once we all were situated, Skye cleared her throat, and looked directly at me. "I think I was instructed to start off with 'Oliver, I owe you an apology.'" She smiled timidly, testing the waters, and when I smiled too, she reached for my hand. I held hers in mine, and she went on. "I was a horrible, horrible bitch and an even worse friend. I'm lucky you will even be in the same room with me at this point, let alone hold my hand in what I hope is forgiveness. I was mean and judgmental and unfair, and I hope you can forgive me for the things I said and the way I treated you. I was wrong, and I'm ashamed and embarrassed for the way I behaved. I put all the wrong things in front of our friendship, and I will never do that again. I love you." Tears were rolling down both our cheeks by the time she finished.

"I love you too, Skye Blue. I'm sorry for the things I said too. Most of them, at least." I winked, and she giggled. "I hope we never fight like that again." We shared a quick chair hug before she took a deep breath and started again.

"Bailey. I don't know where to begin." She angled her body in the chair to face my beautiful girlfriend fully. "So many things happened when Oliver started seeing you. My life literally fell apart. In one quick turn of events, I lost my best friend and the career I'd been working toward for years. I put the crosshairs on your back because it was the logical place to aim. I'm sorry for the petty, hateful things I said behind your back. I fell into the trappings of office gossip and game playing, and now"—she thumbed over her shoulder toward the door— "I just heard you say you did it to help me. Obviously, that was one of many reasons, I understand that, but why not just say something? Let me in on the plan and let me be part of the solution?"

"You have to understand, Skye," Bailey responded. "Even though people think they have a great poker face and they can react in a natural way, nothing replaces the organic process. And unfortunately, that's what we needed to happen in this entire situation. And it wasn't just up to me to decide. All the players in this game agreed it was in everyone's best interest to let things play out as they naturally would have if Mayor Roberts put me in the city manager position and all the interoffice politics played out as they had.

"If you had taken that position, so much evidence would have been altered or destroyed all together. By me taking the position and giving Roberts the impression I was already privy to everything William had been up to, he was lazy and didn't bother covering his tracks or changing his behavior at all. The hardest part was coming to work every day and watching his disgusting antics go on right under everyone's noses."

Skye shook her head in agreement. "It makes sense. And I can't thank you enough for saving my career. When all the dust settles, that's what it boils down to. You saved my political life. If I had been appointed by Roberts, I'd be in lockup right now, because no doubt, my signature would have been on something over these past few weeks, and then I'd be under investigation too. My career would be over before it even got started. All because I think I know better than everyone else. So, I thank you. I hope you can find it in your heart to forgive me. Oliver is a very lucky man to have you in his life."

Skye looked at me and smiled, and continued, "But I have to say, you are a very lucky woman to have him in yours. He is an amazing, kind, loving, and giving soul. He has the capacity to love way beyond himself, and if you are the very lucky person he decides to bestow that upon, you should consider yourself one of the luckiest humans that ever existed. All the rotten, deceitful things William did to lose your faith in men? This one will make you forget in the blink of an eye. Please cherish him. Take care of him. Love him with all that you have in your heart. He deserves nothing less." She wiped more tears from her cheeks when she finished.

Then Skye stood up and walked toward Bailey's desk. "I'll leave my resignation here. I trust you will see the right person gets it?"

"Skye?" Bailey stopped her as she reached the door. She walked over to her desk and picked up the folder Skye had set down. "Why don't you hold on to this? Keep your options open."

"But I..." Skye protested.

"You know the saying from Alexander Graham Bell? When one door closes, another one opens?" Bailey walked over to where Skye still stood in the doorway and handed her the folder.

Skye took the papers, looking quizzically to the other woman. "Yeah?"

"Perfect." With a gentle nudge, she pushed her into the hallway and closed the door behind her. Leaning against the shut panel, she grinned toward me.

My smile matched hers as I strode over to her, pressed her flat against the door and kissed her until we were both breathless.

"I love you," I whispered against her lips.

"I love you too, Oliver. This has been the best day."

"Yeah, it has. Let's go home and celebrate." I grabbed her bag off the back of her chair while she took her coat off the coatrack in the corner.

"I like that plan," she said while I held the jacket for her to slip on.

"I know just the way too." I kissed the shell of her ear while she fastened the buttons of her coat.

"Oh? Do tell!"

"I was thinking we might make your fantasy come true." Her back was still to me, and I waited for my words to sink in.

She thought for a minute and then looked to me with a quick snap of her head. "Do you mean...? Are you talking about what I said the other night?" A smile tugged at her lips.

"Have you changed your mind?" We flipped off the lights and made sure the door to her office was locked with a quick test of the closed handle.

"No. But. I mean, you said someday. I didn't think you meant by the end of the week." She laughed.

"Well, you never know. These things might take practice. Try, try, try again. I just think we should probably get to practicing. You know, show some effort."

Bailey's smile could've lit up the entire city block, and that was all my heart needed to know to be certain I was making the right decision. I'd given it a lot of thought since we talked that first night, and I had never been more sure about spending my life with someone or having a family with a woman than I was with Bailey.

"What are your thoughts on getting married again?" I quizzed as we walked hand in hand to the parking structure. Fall nights meant the sun was long gone, and the ocean air brought dampness into the city atmosphere.

"I wouldn't be opposed to it." She smiled shyly and then stopped in her tracks. "Are you asking me to marry you, Oliver?"

"No. When I ask you, you're going to know it, woman. Shit. I have bigger ideas than a parking garage!" We both continued toward the car, now one of the few remaining in the structure.

"Trust me, I've seen some of your ideas. I can attest to them being big." We got into the X5, and I cranked up the heat. We were on the freeway in no time, holding hands and listening to the local news outline Bailey's press conference in the background.

Happily-ever-afters come in all shapes and sizes. Ours was a work in progress, but I was confident we were on our way to making it happen. Bailey had once told me her days of planning things down to the very detail were behind her, and in general, I would agree. I had every intention of making her plan out the details of a wedding, though, and this time, when she said "I do," it would be for love, happiness, family, and forever.

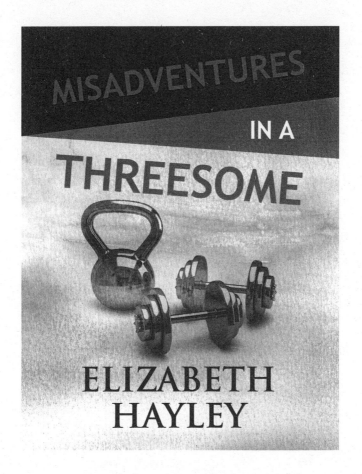

MISADVENTURES

IN A

THREESOME

ELIZABETH
HAYLEY

Keep reading for an excerpt!

EXCERPT FROM
MISADVENTURES IN A THREESOME

The first time Jasmine Pritchett interviewed for a job, she was fourteen years old and had thought getting paid minimum wage at the local pizza shop would result in her financial independence. It hadn't. And now, at twenty-five, she found herself in a similar predicament: hoping *this* job would result in financial independence. Thankfully, according to one of the owners of the gym, the position paid significantly more than her minimum-wage pizza shop gig.

The man who now sat across a desk from her had introduced himself as Wilder. He was at least a foot taller than her five-four frame and had enough muscle on his body to make him appear even larger than he already was. From behind a pair of reading glasses he'd put on when they'd sat down, he studied her résumé closely. His light hair was shaved close on the sides into a high fade, and the longer top was styled into textured, messy spikes. As he played with his bottom lip, she noticed the nuanced hues of his short beard: blonds to light reds with a few grays even. She wondered how old the man was.

She also wondered if he was thinking she was underqualified for the trainer position. Surely she was.

Though she had several fitness certifications, Jasmine's experience in the field was minimal, as was her education. She didn't hold a bachelor's degree or even an associate's in sports science—or in anything, for that matter.

What she did have that she hoped would give her a leg up on her competition was persistence. She'd never been one to retreat just because the opposing army seemed stronger. And she didn't plan on backing down this time either. If these men questioned her abilities, she'd prove herself one way or another. Even if it involved getting the larger of the two into a firefly pose, which—now that she thought about it—she'd actually like to witness.

Jasmine smiled at the other man who had introduced himself earlier as Maddox. There wasn't much else to do, since Wilder was still reading her résumé. She wasn't sure if that was a good sign or a bad one, but she hoped that if they weren't interested, they wouldn't have bothered calling her in the first place. She'd only been here ten minutes, and things already felt unbearably awkward.

♦ ♦ ♦ ♦

Maddox wasn't sure what to do with his eyes. Wilder had been looking at this woman's résumé for at least a full five minutes, which way too long, especially since Maddox assumed Wild would've looked at her résumé *before* calling Jasmine in for an interview.

Now Maddox was stuck exchanging glances with the dark-haired woman as if the two of them were participating in some sort of reverse staring game. The instant the two made eye contact, it was a race to see who could look away first without appearing as though they were doing so. Maddox cleared his throat and held out his hand to Wild—an act intended to move the interview along. Maddox also wanted something to look at other than Jasmine's dark-green eyes, which had already transfixed him.

He took notice of the way her fingers rubbed against her palms as if they had a mind of their own, and he wondered if she was nervous. He hoped it was the silence that had her uneasy and not Maddox's stern demeanor. There was no doubt the army had hardened him, changed Maddox in a way that caused him to stay on guard when he didn't need to, and unfortunately that backfired on him from time to time—especially around people who didn't know him.

"You have a pretty extensive résumé, Ms. Pritchett." Wilder offered her a smile before handing the paper to Maddox, for which he was thankful.

"I do?"

Her reply sounded like a question, and Maddox could only guess that was because her previous work experience ranged from helping the elderly with chores to cutting hair to selling essential oils. Thankfully she did have a few certifications that qualified her to coach classes at Transform, or Maddox would've wondered why the hell Wild had called her in. Though the picture of her at the top of the page would have answered that question.

"I mean, thank you, Mister..."

"Vaughn," he said. "Wilder Vaughn. You can just call me Wild."

Jasmine nodded and gave him a small smile. "You can call me Jaz." Awkward silence followed until she broke it. "Does your personality live up to your name?"

♦ ♦ ♦ ♦

The question wasn't new to Wild, but the way she'd asked it was. Like the idea that he might be a little bit crazy both intrigued and frightened her. Usually comments of the sort had come from high school teachers or previous employers. A time or two it had come with a warning from a date's father, but never from someone interviewing for a job in *his* gym.

"Depends," he answered honestly. "If by wild, you mean fun, then yes. And between the two of us"—he gestured to Maddox—"I'm definitely the funner one." He was sure the comment would've earned him a solid punch to the arm if a prospective employee weren't sitting across from them.

"'Funner' isn't a word," Maddox corrected.

Wild rolled his eyes at Maddox, which made him laugh. That always did. Sometimes a raised eyebrow would follow when Maddox caught Wilder talking excitedly about getting matching Hawaiian shirts and tickets to Jimmy Buffett or stumbled around crashing into furniture in their apartment because he'd had too much tequila at Max's Public House after work...or starting demolition on their gym because his business partner hadn't yet hired the contractor they'd agreed on.

Mad's words always said *Stop, you're acting like a fool*, or something of the sort, but his eyes said something entirely different. They settled somewhere between *What am I gonna do with you?* and *I'm only intervening because I care.* That usually made Wild that much more eager to do whatever it was he'd been up to because he didn't want to offset the delicate balance of their friendship—a balance each man contributed to. Maddox would never let Wild do anything...well, too wild. And Wilder would never let Maddox become so serious about life that he wouldn't enjoy living it. Wild hoped, at least.

"I'm more fun, then," Wilder said. "And also more ambitious. If I had it my way, I would've expanded the gym and hired someone like you months ago," he said to Jasmine.

Now Maddox rolled *his* eyes. "*Ambitious* is one way to put it. Though I'd probably go with *crazy.*"

◆ ◆ ◆ ◆

There was something Jaz liked about the way the men looked at each other—like there was a trust and camaraderie between them that she hadn't experienced with another person. The realization saddened her a bit, but she wouldn't let it show. Witnessing it—though she wasn't a *part* of it—was still somehow satisfying. "Mad and Wild," she said. "Cute."

Maddox raised a dark eyebrow at her. "Did you just call us cute?"

It probably wasn't the most professional moment of Jasmine's life, but it certainly wasn't the most *un*professional one either. Though she wasn't sure that realization justified the remark. "Is that bad? If it helps, I meant it as a compliment."

She hadn't noticed Maddox's smooth, tan skin and pink

lips before, but they now did things to her that she'd rather not be thinking about during an interview. She wondered what his ethnicity was, because she couldn't put her finger on it. Not that it mattered. Biology—and the gym—had been good to him. That was for sure.

"That's how *I* took it," Wild said, drawing her attention back to him.

She was sure these guys had never been called cute in an interview before today, and the fact that she'd been the one to break that streak made her blush a bit, though she hoped they didn't notice.

"We're looking for someone who can teach a variety of group classes, Ms. Pritchett," Maddox said.

"Please. Jaz."

"Jaz," Maddox repeated, his tone no-nonsense, and the look he gave her was intense. "We already have someone for kickboxing, spin, and Zumba. We were thinking of adding some yoga or Pilates, possibly something else, though we aren't sure what yet. Guess it depends on what the new instructor's qualified to do. We're in the process of renovating the space currently, and we'd like to expand the variety of what we offer and, in turn, expand our clientele. I see you've taught yoga and have a few other certifications. Why don't you tell us a little bit about what you're willing to teach?"

Anything that pays the bills was what Jaz wanted to say, but she went with, "Yoga, for sure. I've taught it for a few years and have recently begun incorporating essential oils into my classes. But I can do Pilates, BODYPUMP, whatever you need really. I'm a Jaz of all trades." She hoped that her pun—and the bright smile she beamed at them—would lessen a little of the tension she felt when Maddox spoke. Wilder hadn't been kidding. His business partner was definitely the more serious one.

Maddox opened his mouth like he was about to reply, but Wilder spoke first. "How'd you like to be on the Transform team, Jaz?"

"You're hiring me?" She couldn't disguise the excitement in her voice, and she didn't want to.

Wild raised an eyebrow at his friend, most likely a silent plea for confirmation that his offer was an acceptable one.

After a long moment, Maddox extended his hand to her. "You're hired," he said sternly but added a nod and a small smile. "You have time for a tour?"

Jasmine took his large hand in hers and gave Maddox a nod of her own, thinking she had time for whatever these men had in store for her.

This story continues in
Misadventures in a Threesome!

ACKNOWLEDGMENTS

A very special thank you to the fabulous team at Waterhouse Press for providing the stage for me to sing my first solo. Thank you to the Night Shift Maniacs, Meredith Wild and Angel Payne, for sprinting and endless words of wisdom. The camaraderie definitely helps make the blank pages seem less daunting, and I truly appreciate your support. Thank you, Martha Frantz and all the sisters of Victoria's Book Secrets, for your support and love. You are the kindest, most caring group of friends a girl could surround herself with.

MORE MISADVENTURES

MORE MISADVENTURES